This is a work of fiction. Similarities to real people, places, or events are entirely coincidental.

FOR BETTER OR WORSE

First edition. July 14, 2021.

Copyright © 2021 Monica Marks.

ISBN: 979-8215768518

Written by Monica Marks.

FOR BETTER OR WORSE
MONICA MARKS

1

For Better or Worse

Emily did her very best to keep the scowl from forming on her lovely face but it was becoming increasingly difficult. She watched her sister through her peripheral vision, her mouth pressed to the lip of the china tea cup.

"You are doing that improperly," Randall growled at Amy from over his periodical. "You must use more pressure."

To Emily's mounting disdain, Amy apologized to her husband and worked more tirelessly at massaging feet as though her sister did not sit by and attempt to enjoy her tea.

How does she perform such an awful task without flinching? I daresay she enjoys it and I can barely stomach this beverage

"What of you, Emily?" Randall asked quite unexpectedly, perhaps sensing his sister-in-law's disdain. "When do you intend to cease with this stubbornness and see yourself wed?"

"Pardon me?" For a moment, Emily thought she had misheard the brazen question but Randall did not falter as he stared at her unblinkingly. It was not the first time he had brought up such a matter but Emily had certainly not anticipated it that evening.

"Randall only wishes for you to find the same happiness we have," Amy interjected, worried that her sister's infamous temper was rising. "You cannot fault us that."

Emily gaped at Amy in disbelief. Could Amy not see to what she had been reduced? Emily wondered what their mother would say to know that her sisters had resigned to lives where they tended to their husbands as if they were no better than common servants. Mary Castor had raised her three daughter without the benefit of a husband, Robert Castor having died one year after Emily's birth. She had never remarried although Emily did not learn until she was much older that her father had been terribly cruel to her mother, a fate that Rachel Castor had never wished upon her own children.

"When you marry," Mary had often told Emily and her two older siblings. "Marry a man who sees you as his partner, not his slave."

Emily had taken the words to heart while Amy and Elsbeth seemed content marrying the first man who asked. Neither had been courted by any other man and both of Emily's brothers-in-law were overbearing, demanding men who treated her sisters with near-disgust. Emily could not fathom wedding herself to such a beast, no matter how much Randall and Peter attempted to see her wed.

They are not my father. They have no bearing on my future.

Unfortunately, Emily knew that the matter was not so simple, not when she lived under the same roof as Randall and Amy.

"You will find yourself an old maid yet," Randall prophesized. "No one will want a woman pass a certain age as a wife if you do not act quickly. What about that Darius fellow from church? He seems to make eyes at you quite a lot."

If possible, Emily's mouth dropped further in shock. She was sure if there were flies about, she would have trapped them all.

"Franklin Darius is a man of fifty!" Emily choked. "With six young children of his own!"

In fact, Franklin Darius had been married and buried two wives before finding himself alone again. It was a small wonder he was looking to a woman over half his age for his next wife, one who would bear him more children and not perish before him. The mere notion made her shudder with repulsion.

"He is a lonely widower," Randall growled, his eyes narrowing meanly as he leaned forward. "The children need a mother."

Emily was unsure which she found more offensive—the idea that she was not suited to be better than a nanny for six rambunctious boys, not her own or the fact that her brother-in-law thought he could use her to improve his business connections through marriage. Emily knew that Franklin Darius was an associate of Randall's, even though her brother-in-law would never admit to using her in such a fashion.

"Then I suggest he employ a governess," Emily snapped back, causing Randall's face to flush with anger. He rose menacingly from his chair to tower over Emily and she did the same, meeting his eyes evenly. Randall was hardly a tall man and met his gaze precisely on level.

"Enough!" Amy breathed, perhaps realizing that her husband intended to raise a hand to her sister. "Emily, why must you be so contrary?"

"I will not continue to house you while you sulk about like a child, Emily Castor!" Randall huffed, not permitting Emily a chance to answer Amy. "You will find a husband, I have decided and it will be Franklin Darius!"

Emily's eyes widened, her mouth twisting into a grimace of disdain.

He has been thinking this for quite some time! She realized. *He was simply biding his time to bring it up in a circumstance such as this. I am made to look unreasonable and he, my savior. Well I do not need saving. When I marry, it will be a man who wishes for a partner, not a chambermaid.*

"I will do nothing of the sort," Emily retorted dismissively. "And there is nothing you can do or say which will change my mind."

The slap came suddenly although Emily had half expected such a blow from Randall. Still, the sting caught her off guard and sent her reeling back, more from shock than pain. A gloved hand rose to her cheek, matched only by the burn of tears in her eyes.

"Randall!" Amy gasped but she made no move to intervene between her sister and husband. Amy looked at Emily, the anger in her face evident.

She is upset with me, not him! Emily thought although why that was stunning, she could not say. Never would she expect Amy nor Elsbeth to take her side, not when there would be hell to pay later with their husbands.

No, Emily was truly alone. It was a fact she had known for quite a long while yet it did not make it any less painful. With their mother gone, there was no one to share in her desire for something more.

"You will do as you are told, Emily or you will find yourself begging for coins in the gutter, I swear!" Randall hissed.

Emily threw her head back defiantly and glared at him, willing herself not to cry. She did not doubt the sincerity of Randall's threat but she would not give him the satisfaction of seeing her falter.

"Then I imagine I shall go searching for a gutter rife with traffic," she retorted. "I am certain it will reflect well on you to have your sister-in-law begging in the street."

Their eyes clashed again but Emily could see the uncertainty shadowing Randall's face as he considered what she had said. Even though he knew he could not throw her onto the streets while he lived well but Emily was also sure she could not depend on his reputation to keep her safe forever. At some point, she would be forced to marry someone of his choosing or move along.

And where would I go?

She had already overextended her welcome with Elsbeth and Peter which was how she had found herself living with Amy. If Randall made good on his threat to see her gone, there would be nowhere else to live.

"You are far too shrewish for your own good," Randall growled at her. "It will be a miracle if anyone would have you with such a tongue. I would not be surprised if Darius changes his mind about marrying you when he realizes your wits do not match your face."

"Please, Emily, do hear him out. Franklin Darius is a good man with means to provide for you. Why would you not—" Amy began to say but Emily had heard quite enough from the pair and she spun to leave.

"Come back here at once!" Randall roared after her. "You have gone too far this time, Emily Castor!"

Yet Emily did not return to the front salon. She had heard quite enough for one afternoon. Never had it been clearer that something needed to be done. She needed to leave New York at once.

~ ~ ~

Stephen heard the clip-clap of the horses hooves before his eyes befell the mail cart approaching but he did not stop his work. There was too much to be done before day's end for him to pause, even though he knew precisely what the cart held for him as it neared his position. It was with some dread he anticipated its arrival.

"Good afternoon, Mr. Meridian," Jackson called, his face gleaming with sweat as he stopped the cart at the fence. "I have mails for you."

"Thank you, Jackson," Stephen said tersely, reluctantly ambling closer to the man to accept the single envelope from his outstretched hand. The postman seemed uncomfortable as though he expected Stephen to say more but he did not and instead turned his attention back to his duties as if to dismiss the mailman without another word.

"Is that from your young lady?" Jackson asked, causing Stephen to eye him again with mounting annoyance.

"I imagine so," Stephen muttered. "Good day, Jackson."

He was hardly in the mood to discuss his impending nuptials with a near-stranger, even if Jackson had been his postman for almost a decade. Perhaps that was why Stephen wished him away. Jackson had seen too much of Stephen's life, matters the rancher wished he could forget.

"Good day, Mr. Meridian."

With a small huff of air, Jackson whipped his horse, urging him along and soon, Stephen was left in peace to peruse the letter he had received from Emily Castor. He looked about, almost as though he expected to be observed by one of the hands but of course the others were minding their own tasks.

Why do I wish someone would distract me from reading this?

The idea was ridiculous. The last letter he had sent had offered a betrothal to the woman out east. She was a good a match as he had found, her letters simple and lacking some of the fanciful notions of romance or adventure he had detected in others he had received. It was what had drawn Stephen to Emily Castor—she seemed determined to come to Montana Territory to work the land, not for the idea of falling in love.

I will never make that mistake again, not after what happened with Catherine.

He shoved the reminder of his former fiancée aside and read the letter Emily had penned, a basic note, accepting the terms of his proposal and explaining that she was prepared to leave immediately.

Once more, Stephen was filled with conflicting emotions, bittersweet and unsettled.

You require a wife and Emily Post will do nicely. There is no reason to consider this more than a simple arrangement beneficial for us both.

Yet as he made his way back into the house, dabbing at the sweat at his brow with a dirty kerchief, he considered that perhaps he was making a mistake, that maybe he did not need a wife at all.

You do, he growled, knowing this very argument well. *What good is it to build a fruitful life without the benefit of a son for whom to pass it along?*

He washed his hands in the kitchen basin before making his way to the study where he instantly began to pen Emily a letter with fare for her to collect a train ticket westbound.

And he wrote faster than he ever had in his life, lest he change his mind.

~ ~ ~

Another may have been deterred by Stephen Meridian's almost brusque mannerisms but Emily found them oddly comforting. He was not rude to her when his farm hand ushered her into the house after retrieving her from the train station that morning. He introduced himself with a cool politeness although Emily did note that he seemed to appraise her through his peripheral vision.

She found herself pleasantly surprised by his attractiveness but she was not one to be fooled by outward appearances. Emily had known many dashing men who were nothing more than insipid and foppish but Stephen was more than merely a handsome man. It was plain to see in this thriving ranch, its well-kept land and healthy livestock. There was something intense and brooding beneath his vivid eyes of blue, two shades darker than her own.

No, it was clear that Stephen Meridian was not the spoiled son of a wealthy man like her brothers-in-law but a man who had worked tirelessly for what he had. Emily was surprised to find that the house was immaculately kept, despite the absence of a woman to cook and clean.

"Have you houses servants?" she heard herself ask and a slight scowl touched Stephen's lips although when he spoke, his voice was kept quite even.

"I had hoped that this union would be a benefit to us both. There is much work to be done on this land, inside and out," he replied. "I am not a frugal man but I do believe in hard work. No, there are no servants."

He paused as though gauging her reaction.

"However," he continued, contemplating his next words carefully. "I would not wish to overwhelm you with chores. Should you find yourself overcome with duties, I would not be opposed to hiring a housekeeper."

Guilt and embarrassment flooded Emily and she shook her head vehemently.

"As I explained in my letters, Mr. Meridian," she said quickly. "I have come here hoping to build upon something. I am certain we might work well...together."

She stressed the word, now watching his face for a response. Stephen seemed to relax, her response apparently the proper one.

"Very well." He nodded toward her trunks. "Is this all you have brought?"

"I have more which I can send for." She did not add that she had not wanted to bring too much, lest she was forced to leave but as she stood in the foyer, she could not help but feel that she had found a home finally. Whether it was because she had left behind the endless ridicule of her family or it was Stephen himself which enabled her to enjoy a modicum of peace, she could not say.

"The pastor will be here in the morning," Stephen explained. "I was unsure at what time your train was to arrive and we must be wed before noon. I will see myself to sleep in the barn tonight."

The notion filled her with confusion.

"The barn?" she echoed. "Whatever for? Surely there are many chambers in this household!"

He cast her a dubious look.

"We are unmarried, Miss Castor," he reminded her but Emily had never heard such a thing. Of course in the east, matters were handled quite differently. Still, she could not in good conscience, permit the master of his house to sleep with the sheep.

Could you imagine Randall or Peter offering such a thing? They would never forfeit the comfort of their own beds to ensure my sisters.

"I will not have you uprooted from your own home," she insisted, causing his eyes to widen. "Perhaps I will see myself to town with a companion. I might find an inn in which to sleep for the night. Have you any woman who might come with me?"

To her shock, Stephen snickered slightly.

"The closest town hasn't an inn for you to stay and Helena is half a day by cart. I assure you, Miss Castor, this arrangement is best."

Emily did not know what to say and instead remained silently standing in her spot.

"Miss Castor, I assure you, this is the way matters are done here," Stephen offered gruffly, seemingly embarrassed himself. "You need not seem so uncomfortable."

"I am not," she answered quickly. "I merely..."

She trailed off and met his eyes for the first time. Unexpectedly, a flush of warmth flooded her body as a fission of energy seemed to transfer between them.

"I am merely getting adjusted," she concluded. "Where might I put my trunks?"

"Charlie will see them to your quarters." He waved his hand toward the hand who had remained nearby and the helper reached for them. "Miss Castor's room is the last at the end of the hall."

Charlie cast his employer an odd look.

"That is not your room, Stephen," the young man chirped, apparently before he could consider his words. Emily watched as Stephen's face flushed crimson.

"I am quite aware, thank you," he barked. "Take her trunks at once!"

Charlie was humiliated but he did as he was told, leaving Emily with a sinking feeling in the pit of her gut.

Does he not intend for us to share a room at all or is it only until we are married under God?

She could not say why but she hoped that the latter was true.

~ ~ ~

The ceremony was blessedly sweet and short, the pastor gone within an hour of his arrival, citing other unions he had to fashion that very morning.

"God bless you both," the reverend muttered before leaving the newlywed couple to eye one another uncertainly.

Stephen had not been expecting Emily to be quite so comely. He tried to tell himself that her attractiveness meant nothing, that she was merely a partner with whom to run ranch matters but he could not help but stare at her delicate features. To his amazement, he saw she returned his cautious stares with ones of her own.

She does not look a lick like Catherine, he realized with some relief. Their coloring was different and undeniably, Emily's bright eyes reflected a warmth that Catherine's never did.

I suppose in hindsight, all that Catherine did was suspect, he reasoned. Stephen wondered why he was thinking about his treacherous former fiancée.

"Shall we get to work?" Emily asked and Stephen realized that several moments of silence had passed. Color tinged his cheeks and he lowered his gaze reluctantly.

"We needn't start at once," he told her. "First, let us eat and discuss our future. We did not have much opportunity to speak yesterday."

That had been mostly his fault. He had felt distinctly uncomfortable in the company of an unattended woman, even if she was his fiancée. Moreover, Emily had been weary from her travels and he had wanted to give her opportunity to rest but all night, he had tossed and turned in the barn loft. It was not until nearly dawn that he realized he was more excited than nervous by the impending marriage and he hoped that his bride-to-be felt the same.

"Of course," Emily said, sounding surprised by his suggestion. "I will prepare us a meal at once."

"I will prepare it," he told her and he did not miss the gape of her mouth.

"You?" she echoed before she could stop herself. "You are able to cook?"

In spite of himself, he smiled.

"As I mentioned, there are no servants to do the chores. I have learned to function quite well on my own."

A stab of sadness hit him as he realized how lonely he had been without knowing it but as he gazed at the lovely face of his new wife, he wondered if that part of his life might be finished.

Perhaps. If I permit it to be.

But the devastation of what Catherine had done could not be easily dismissed and while he could not deny that Emily Castor was already exceeding his expectations, he had once thought the same of another woman.

"Come along, Mrs. Meridian," he said, extending his arm for her and she took it without hesitation.

Her touch emboldened him and they continued into the kitchen where he guided her to a chair.

"Are you quite sure I cannot do anything?" Emily asked, sounding nervous. "I do not feel quite right doing absolutely nothing."

"You might regale me with tales about your family," Stephen suggested as he fired the stove. He did not miss the appreciative look which Emily cast him until he mentioned her family. A frown twisted on her beautiful face and she looked at her hands.

"I have two sisters. My mother and father have gone to heaven."

"I am very sorry to know that," Stephen replied sympathetically. "My father is in poor health. He stays with my sister in Butte but we will go soon. He will be happy to know I have married before he, too, meets with God."

Emily peered at him speculatively.

"You did not tell anyone that you were marrying?" she asked curiously. It was Stephen's turn to look away, his own lips curling downward.

"No," he growled in a darker tone than he had intended.

I would not be the subject of ridicule again if this union did not occur.

A long, heavy silence befell the space between them and Stephen busied himself at the stove, angered that he had permitted Catherine back into his thoughts.

"Mr. Meridian?"

They both turned at the sound of a man's voice entering the house.

"Who in God's name could that be?" Stephen muttered, wiping his hands as he moved around the counter.

James Birkenstock appeared suddenly before him and Stephen started in surprise to see the banker.

"Mr. Birkenstock," Stephen muttered. "I was not expecting you."

"I was merely in the area and…" the dapper man trailed off, his eyes falling upon Emily who had risen hastily. "Ah, forgive me. I did not realize you were entertaining at such an early hour."

The leer in the man's voice was unmistakable, his eyes trained uncouthly upon her face unblinkingly.

"This is my wife, Mrs. Emily Meridian." Apprehension mounted in his gut as James strode forward to take Emily's hand.

"Your wife! I had no idea you had married, Meridian! Good on you!"

He did not look at Stephen once as he pressed Emily's hand to his lips.

"Charmed, Mrs. Meridian. I daresay you are much comelier than the last one." He chuckled rudely and Stephen saw a shadow fall over Emily's face.

"The last one?" she murmured. Stephen bristled.

"Why have you come, Mr. Birkenstock. As you can see, we are about to eat."

"I do not mind if I do stay!" James chortled, deliberately taking Stephen's word as an invitation. "My word, a wife."

A tongue jutted out to lick his lower lip and the banker continued to keep his gaze fixed on Emily who looked away, a blush tinging her cheeks.

Anger bubbled inside Stephen.

"And look at you, doing women's work!" James laughed merrily. "Is that not the very purpose of a wife?"

"Pardon me," Emily said stiffly. "I have a matter which requires my attention."

Stephen nodded curtly.

"Hurry back, now," James sighed as she gathered her skirts and slipped through the back door into the fields beyond. It was only then that Stephen had the banker's full attention.

"You scoundrel! So soon after the last?"

"Do not think me rude, Mr. Birkenstock but we do have a rather pressing morning. What brings you this way?"

James smiled coyly.

"I imagine there is much that can be done with such a comely article," James chortled but Stephen's frown only deepened.

"Mr. Birkenstock!"

"Yes, yes. I have come because I have word on the plot to the north. It is for sale if you wish to acquire it."

Stephen's pulse was racing.

"Fine," he said stiffly. "I will come into Helena and we will discuss the numbers."

"Or I might stay for a day or two and we might go through the papers here."

Stephen eyed him with wariness.

"You have the papers with you?"

"Of course. I would not come so far without them. Of course, if I had known you had such a lovely wife, I would have come much sooner. When did you marry her?"

Stephen's jaw tightened.

"Today," he muttered, wishing that the banker would leave. Yet he had wanted to purchase land on the adjoining properties for years now and Stephen knew if he sent James away, he might lose the sale.

"I wonder what Mrs. Fielding will say when she learns of this," James murmured, his eyes glimmering with a sinister amusement.

"I could not care less what Catherine has to say on the matter," Stephen spat with bitter venom. The banker whooped and claimed the seat which Emily had occupied.

"Hear hear!" he agreed. "A whore, she was."

Stephen's jaw locked in anger. Regardless of his feelings toward Catherine, he did not like hearing her spoken of so poorly. Still, he held his tongue. He only needed to sign the papers and James Birkenstock would be on his way.

"Leave the papers," he said. "I will look them over and return them to you tomorrow...in Helena."

"No need, my boy. I will spend the night and be on my way tomorrow. I am already here, after all and it will permit me more time to know your bride."

Stephen could not imagine why James Birkenstock, a married man and father of four, would need to know his young wife at all but he again said nothing.

"As you wish," Stephen replied grimly. "I will find a room for you."

James leaned across the table, his mouth curling into an ugly smile under his greying moustache.

"Wherever did you find this one?"

Stephen could not understand the banker's fascination with his bride but he decidedly did not like it.

"She hails from New York."

"Oh! One of those matrimonial column brides, then?"

Stephen did not answer as he turned back to the stove, feeling James' eyes on his back.

"Well, wherever you found her, I daresay I hope she prove to be more virtuous than the fallen woman you almost married."

Stephen remained silent but in his heart, he had to agree that he felt the same.

I need not worry about Emily, he thought. *She would never break our marital vows...would she?*

Yet with a sinking feeling in his gut, Stephen realized he had thought the very same of Catherine before she had become pregnant during their betrothal...with the child of another man.

~ ~ ~

From the very moment James Birkenstock had walked into the house, the feeling of peace was stolen from Emily. She felt as if one of her brothers-in-law had entered her life again and sucked the air from her lungs.

There were many similarities between James and her sisters' husbands, after all. They carried themselves with the same foppishness, same arrogance. There was nothing earthly about James Birkenstock, as if he thought himself much better than her self-made husband.

All about the banker bothered Emily and she wished for nothing more than for him to leave their land and never return.

She made herself scarce for the rest of the day, the meal she was intended to have with her new husband, forsaken. Instead, the two men discussed business, leaving Emily feeling alienated as she wandered about the grounds, finding tasks to keep her occupied.

When she returned to the house in the late afternoon, Stephen was nowhere in sight but James Birkenstock sat in the study, smoking a pipe. The scent made her stomach lurch.

"Ah, there you are, Mrs. Meridian," the older man cooed in a tone one might expect to use with a child. "Stephen has gone looking for you."

"Has he?" Emily felt guilty.

"Do come and entertain me," James insisted as he read the uncertainty in her face as she decided what to do next. "It is terribly rude to leave a guest unattended, if you do not mind me saying so."

Emily had no desire to sit with this man, unaccompanied but she reasoned that he was a friend of her husband's.

You are a married woman now. This is a part of your duties.

"Of course," she replied, forcing a smile and glided further into the study. "Have you concluded your business then?"

An unbecoming leer formed on Emily's lips and instantly, her stomach churned.

"Perhaps," James replied. "Perhaps you and I could discuss business of our own."

Emily froze before him, the smile fading from her lips.

"I know little of the ways of ranching yet," she replied tautly although she was quite certain that was not the business to which he referred. "Those are matters best left to discuss with my husband."

James rose, his face mere centimeters from hers. Instantly, she was reminded of Randall and the power he attempted to exude.

"Oh, but I can think of far more interesting matters to discuss than ranching, can you not?"

Emily stepped back but that did not stop the banker from reaching forward to grasp her arm.

"You are far too beautiful to waste away on a ranch," he murmured, drawing her closer. Emily tried to wrest away but James was surprisingly strong for such a slight man of a certain age.

Before Emily's temper had proper time to flare, the sound of a gasp wafted toward them from the doorway and she managed to wrench free, spinning to see Stephen's look of disbelief.

"What is the meaning of this?" he demanded, his voice barely a rasp. Emily did not have an opportunity to speak before James boomed out a laugh.

"Why, you should not be surprised, Stephen. You already know what kind of women you attract. They are clearly all the same. She basically threw herself at me when she realized I was a banker. You cannot fault the woman—shameless as she might be."

Emily's mouth parted in shock.

"I did nothing of the sort!" she hissed, whipping back around to stare at James in dismay. "You grabbed me!"

Her eyes darted back toward her husband but he had spun away to storm from the house.

"You are despicable!" she growled at the banker. "I have half a mind to strike your arrogant face."

James chortled at the thought.

"You would cost your husband a great deal of land if you did," he replied, reaching for her again. "You would do him a better service to appease me. He is already angry, whether or not we finish what we started—"

He did not finish his sentence as Emily's hand snaked out to slap him clear across his cheeks, her hand leaving an undeniable print. For the first time, he lost the smirk, his eyes darkening furiously.

"How dare you!" he choked. "You will pay dearly for this!"

But Emily was already gone, chasing her husband into the yard where she looked about for him desperately.

"Stephen!" she called out and as she did, a rumble of thunder echoed her word. It sent shivers through her, as though God was forewarning her of what was to come.

"Stephen, please," she begged him. "I did nothing wrong."

"I know," he replied and Emily shrieked with fright when he appeared behind her.

She whirled about to stare at him.

"Then why did you leave in such a rush of anger?" she demanded, searching his face. He smiled wanly at her but she could clearly read the pain in his eyes.

"I had to leave before I lost control on Birkenstock. I would not want blood shed in the study."

Relief flooded her body and the first droplets of rain began to fall between them.

"I would never betray my wedding vows," she promised him. "But I fear I may have cost you a plot of land."

"If it means getting that wretched bastard out of our home, I could not care less," Stephen replied and Emily was certain her heart was going to implode with affection for him. What man had she ever known who would say such a thing and mean every word he spoke? Yet Emily had no doubt Stephen was sincere.

"Your wife is a harlot, Meridian," James muttered, stalking out of the house. "You would do right to annul this marriage before—"

Again, the banker was unable to finish his thought, Stephen's fist making contact with James' jaw, sending the man reeling back into the house and onto his back.

"You would do right to see yourself off this property and never show your face again," Stephen hissed. "I would not like to tell your wife what I have witnessed here today. I am told she is a jealous woman."

James balked at the threat and he managed to amble to his feet, albeit unsteadily.

"You have made a grave mistake!" he hissed. "Mark my words—"

"I would say you are fixing for another kiss," Stephen interjected, his eyes flashing with anger. "Good day, sir."

James clamped his mouth closed and stormed toward his carriage, brushing off his his topcoat as he moved, muttering to himself. It was not until the horse finally disappeared down the laneway that the couple turned to look at one another, exhaling in unison.

"I came here, hoping to escape men like Mr. Birkenstock," Emily muttered miserably. "But perhaps I attract precisely that sort."

"You have attracted me," Stephen corrected her and Emily's heart swelled as she met his eyes. "I do not know if that is to your benefit or detriment. My last fiancée did not think me enough."

"Your last fiancée was a fool who did not appreciate a good, honest man," Emily replied without hesitation. She had gleaned that there was a past which had shamed him, one involving a woman but that had no bearing on her.

"I am pleased you think so," he murmured, reaching for her hands. He pulled her closed and smiled at her warmly. She did not return his smile.

"Have we made a mistake, Stephen? What of the land?"

He chuckled kissed her forehead softly.

"I made no mistake for once in my life," he replied. "Of that, I am certain."

Warmth swept through Emily like a wave as she realized he was not speaking of the property at all but about her.

~ ~ ~

The winter was colder than Emily had expected but it was difficult to feel particularly chilled bundled under the thick of blankets which Stephen had piled upon her.

"Are you well? Have some water," he recited. The entire journey, he had uttered the same words over and over. If Emily did not love him quite so much, she might have become annoyed.

"You must stop fussing!" she laughed, shooing the waterskin aside. "I am quite content, in fact."

"Are you certain? We will be in Butte very shortly."

"Then you must prepare your words and stop wasting them on my well-being," Emily teased. "You have much to tell your father and sister."

Happiness colored Stephen's face and he nodded, a smile touching his lips.

"I have written about you," he reminded her. "You are already well-loved."

"I imagine any woman would be well-loved after Catherine," Emily commented dryly but Stephen shook his head.

"No, Emily, not any woman," he corrected. "The only woman who has captured both my heart and soul exclusively. Catherine's betrayal was a gift from God. If she had not done what she had done, I would never have found you—my one true love."

The words gave Emily a heady feeling, the sincerity of them overwhelming her.

"I feel the same about you, my darling," she whispered, their eyes locking. From the seclusion of the carriage's cab, they shared a long, sweet kiss.

The horses slowed and they pulled apart.

Stephen cast her a nervous look.

"Are you quite sure you are prepared for this?" he asked and she giggled, cupping his cheek with a gloved hand.

"I look forward to it," she assured him again. "Your father will be beside himself when he hears the news."

Stephen smiled.

"Indeed. What man would not want to hear that he is going to be a grandfather for the first time?"

He lowered his hands over her tumescent belly before meeting her eyes again.

"Thank you, Emily."

"Whatever for?"

"For reminding me how to love."

LIFT ME UP

Maggie referred to her split with James as "The Break-Up". He had been the star football player on the varsity team. She had known him all throughout junior high and high school where he had always been the star athlete.

The guy every girl wanted and she got him.

Their relationship had been tumultuous from the start. She blamed herself at first. Her own feelings of inadequacy and insecurity led her to believe that he had all the answers.

It did seem like he had all the answers. The star quarterback on the team that always made the right decisions. Always come through in the clutch and never let his team down.

Only this did not spill over into his personal relationships. James had that mantel of "you're going places" labeled on him since junior high school. His own parents never accepted Maggie, particularly his father.

Maggie never forgot the conversation she had once with James. She should have been able to read the tea leaves.

"Is your Dad always that quiet?" Maggie asked one day after she had dinner over at James' house.

"He doesn't want me to date," James said. "Thinks that all women are users and that you are only with me because I am going to the pros. He told me when I was young, 'If you get a girl pregnant, you're marrying the bitch.'"

Maggie could only shake her head. "Creep."

"You don't have to talk to him if you don't want to."

"I won't."

"He just doesn't want me to date anyone."

"So what , you're just going to do what your Dad says?"

"No, of course not," James said. "I love you. Absolutely adore you. Why would I follow the lead of someone who has had failed relationships their whole life?"

A week after that conversation, James broke up with Maggie.

Maggie cursed her poverty as she stood washing her hands in the soiled kitchen. Roaches huddled in the gap between the back splash and the flaking plaster wall. She took out her pesticide and sprayed them but the liquid just sputtered out, all used up.

Maggie had always taken the bus to school. The long yellow beast of a machine had carried her through childhood; red vinyl seats had cradled her through new friendships, a broken heart, and life changing decisions.

She walked faster when she saw the line of anxious teens waiting for their ride. Her chapped hands smoothed the brilliant blue shirt that declared her an employee of Sam's Sushi, and caressed the rounding bump of her stomach. Only a few months ago, she would have been standing in that line, worrying about a math test or holding hands with her boyfriend, or making plans to go shopping that weekend. Nobody looked at her as she pushed through the queue of children; they were all focused on their phones (a luxury that she could no longer afford) or were chattering to each other about whatever regular high-schoolers thought about.

The baby was due in five months, one week, and four days. That made it almost three months since the "Break Up", and two months, three weeks since her parents had told her exactly what she would have to do to stay in their good graces.

Sam's was only a few blocks away from her only slightly run-down apartment that (with the help of some well-intentioned college gift money) she'd been able to rent. The neighborhood wasn't the greatest—but then, nobody would even think about touching a pregnant teenager; in fact, more often than not, the shady-looking boys that hung around in dark alleys were the ones that carried her purse and walked her home at night. The fish wasn't the freshest—but Maggie's morning sickness had faded with the first trimester, and she hadn't been even *slightly* nauseated since the end of her twelfth week.

She made it to work on time and pushed her way through the line of customers there to get a free cup of morning coffee that came with the purchase of a Sam's Specialty Breakfast Roll. The time-stamp machine whirred furiously to life as she clocked in and tied on her crisp black apron.

"Good morning, girly," Sam himself called as she waddled forward, tray of sushi platters balanced carefully on her arm. "Been taking your vitamins?"

Maggie grinned up at the large Polynesian man and nodded. "They're awful," she told him. "Like horse pills."

"But you feel good, eh?" Sam laughed and sliced a slab of tuna fish in half. "Not like that Rob Perkins."

Maggie perked up. "He's here today?"

Sam shook his head. "Yes. He's in the back, prepping our soy sauce jugs for the day. You been asking about him a lot, girly."

"Well," Maggie shifted on the balls of her feet and caressed her belly. "He seems nice."

"He's been here for a week, and you think he's nice."

"He doesn't ask questions, Sam," Maggie rolled her eyes. "And best of all, he didn't try to touch my stomach without asking."

"Oh, how low the bar has fallen."

"Hey, I can afford to be picky," Maggie grinned and gestured at her tray. "Which table is this for?"

"Number five. Be careful—they're drunk."

Drunk, but not violent—thank goodness. Maggie had set out all four plates of sushi before one of them even lifted his shaggy head up off of the cheap plastic counter-top to thank her and press a wad of dollar bills into her hand. The next hour was made up purely of coffee refills, order taking, and order delivering. The only other waitress that

Sam employed had come down with the flu, so Maggie was on her own—swollen ankles and all—until the pre-lunch lull hit and she was able to steal a stool from the bar while Sam made a run across the street to buy a case of wasabi from the wholesale foods store.

She sat there, hands over her belly, and watched Rob's back while he washed dishes. He'd somehow escaped the terrifying onslaught that was Sam's uniform campaign, and wore only a thin white t-shirt, tight blue jeans, and heavy black boots. Sweat beaded at the nape of his neck—the A/C had broken about the time he'd been hired, something that an early spring had made regrettable—and made his spiked hair seem even darker than it was.

He had one tattoo—an incredibly lifelike dragon—that wound out from beneath his shirt, down his bulging bicep and veined forearm before spitting inked flame out over the knuckles of the hand that clutched a sponge.

He was incredibly efficient, Maggie realized as she watched him dunk plates, scrub them roughly, dip them into clean water, and then place them, dripping, onto the rack beside the sink. Not exactly a conversationalist, but definitely a hard worker. She pushed her stool back and waddled over to where he stood.

"I'll dry," she said.

"Sit down," he growled, and scrubbed at another dish.

"I'm bored." Maggie picked up a cloth and reached for a plate. "Besides, I'm fine."

"You need a break," he said, and pushed her hand away with the sopping fingers of his own. "Sit down."

"Oh my God," Maggie groaned. "I'm pregnant, not dying. I can handle washing a couple dishes. Maggie Junior can deal with it."

"If you want to do something, you can color code toothpicks."

"While sitting down?"

"While sitting down."

"Come on, Rob."

He stopped scrubbing, and turned so that the pair of foggy blue eyes that normally hid behind drooping eyelids momentarily froze Maggie.

"If I get you a chair," he said. "And if you promise to use it, I'll let you dry."

"I knew it!" Maggie clapped her hands. "You're just a big softie after all."

"Hey," he pointed a dripping finger at her. "Those toothpicks still need sorting. Don't tempt me, Christensen."

"Oh *no*," Maggie feigned horror as she watched Rob pull a stool over to beside the sink. "Not *toothpicks*." She sat down and selected a clean rag from the pile on the counter.

Rob shook his head and went back to cleaning his dishes.

After Maggie's shift, she dug her tote—empty of anything but her apartment keys and a warm jacket—out from the top shelf of the walk-in freezer and bid a cheerful goodbye to Sam and Rob. While she was very nearly a full time worker, and made a substantial profit in tips besides, her age still prevented her from working as many hours as the legal adults.

She walked along the cracked sidewalk, making a quick stop at the nearest convenience store to obtain some much craved ice cream before continuing on and descending into her small basement apartment to microwave dinner and go to bed.

Mornings were hard. With pregnancy had come swollen joints and prickly headaches that made waking up difficult. To Maggie, the one-roomed apartment seemed to be constantly frozen despite the warm weather, and completed her morning routine—uniform change, hair, makeup and all—wrapped in her comforter. She was surprised to hear a knock on her door. None of her friends from the pre-baby days had ever bothered to visit, she'd never bothered to let her parents know where she'd settled...Sure, she'd had the occasional evangelist (always looking to save her from her sins, but never offering to really *help*) and salespeople, but neither of those ever made such strong, self-assured noise.

She shuffled the few yards to the front door and peered curiously through the peephole before pulling it open.

"What are you doing here?" she asked pleasantly as Rob blinked down at her. He was wearing a black shirt today, and the seemingly permanent stubble that occupied the lower half of his face looked decidedly shorter than normal.

"I thought I'd give you a ride," he said. "If you want."

"Uh," Maggie swallowed and Rob shoved his hands into the deep pockets of his worn, oil-stained jeans. "I mean, sure. Wait here while I grab my purse."

"It's cold," he said as he hunched over and slid through the squat door frame. "Is your heat off?"

"I think it's more that the air conditioner is always on," Maggie said as she tucked her jacket, then her keys, into a Gucci knockoff. "Landlord says there's nothing wrong. I can't figure out what's up. So I make do."

"Seriously?"

Maggie shrugged as she slid the purse onto her shoulder and gave her belly a reassuring pat. "Rent's cheap."

Rob sighed and held the door open for her. "Listen," he said as she climbed into the passenger seat of his beat up old pickup truck. "Do you—I mean, I'll come take a look at it sometime. I mean, I'm more of a mechanic than an electrician, but...I mean..."

"That would be great," Maggie said, and buckled her seat belt as he revved the engine and they roared down the street. "I'd really like that."

"No worries," Rob said.

She noticed that that phrase seemed to be his mantra 'no worries.' Her own life was now anything but.

They drove in silence for a few blocks until they passed the bus stop with all of the people waiting.

"I can't believe you take the bus every day. I mean, what if something happened."

"Like what?"

"I don't know."

"Like what if I get so fat I step on the buss and flatten the tire?"

"Yeah," he laughed. "Like that."

Maggie liked Rob's laugh and his smile. He hardly did any of either.

"What are you plans?" he asked. "I mean when the baby is born."

"What do you mean?"

"I mean are you still going to work at the restaurant?"

"Yeah, of course. I am not going to go on welfare if that is what you mean."

"No."

"The father isn't going to help me. That is for sure. But I'll make it. Trust me. I'll make it. I'll show them all and we'll be fine. We may not have tons of money or live in a golden palace but we'll be fine."

Rob nodded his head as he turned the corner. "I think you're going to be a good mother."

"Thanks."

"Do you know if it is going to be a boy or girl?"

"I don't know. Of course, they can tell me but I want it to be a surprise. I'm old fashioned that way. At least, I have to be old-fashioned in *something*."

Work was slower that day—Tuesdays always were, for some reason—but there were just as many dishes to wash...and dry. Sam had agreed that Maggie could help if, as Rob had suggested, she kept her butt on a chair the whole time, so she was able to help as well. It was nice, she thought later, after Rob had dropped her off at her apartment and made her promise to wait for him to pick her up again the next day. He wasn't the most talkative of dishwashers, but she took care of that for the most part. And besides, it was nice to have a friend again.

That became the pattern for the rest of the week—Rob gave her rides, Maggie talked his ear off and dried dishes. She told him the Friday—her day off—would be best if he was serious about taking a look at her air conditioner, and he told her that he never joked about "stuff like that."

Maggie wondered if that was a general phrase, or if it applied to her in particular.

He arrived promptly at eight o'clock on Friday morning, and Maggie—still decked out in her fuzzy maternity-wear pajamas—opened the door and asked him if he was insane.

"I wanted to make sure that I had enough time," he said, and rubbed a thumb across his dragon tattoo. "Just in case."

"I'm not even dressed, Perkins."

"So?" He shrugged. "You do your thing, I'll do mine. Just try not to check me out." And then he winked.

"Fine," Maggie huffed, and shuffled back to make her bed. "The A/C is behind the door down that skinny little hall."

"Thanks," he said, and pried the door open. "How old are you?"

"Seventeen, almost eighteen," she recited, straightening her sheets. "You?"

"Twenty. How are you renting this place?"

"Landlord's a little on the shady side. Lets me pay cash." Maggie glanced behind her to make sure that he was still in the electric room and hurriedly began changing into street clothes. "But it's only until Maggie Junior shows up."

"What'll you do then?"

"I don't know," she said, and sat down in the old wicker chair that took up the corner of her room beside her bed. "I can't go back home—mom and dad'll make me put her up for adoption or something, and I don't want that. Why are you working at Sam's?"

"Garage went out of business." Something clanged. "I'm looking for a new job, but while I do, Sam offered me a little something to help pay the rent. Why do you think your parents are so against having a grand kid?"

"They didn't want me to have her at all," Maggie said. "That's why I came here. So they wouldn't..."

"Ah."

"You found something?"

"Almost. Come here."

Maggie pushed herself to her feet and walked down the hall to the little room that held the water heater, and heating and cooling system.

"See," Rob was standing on his tip toes. "The wire that's meant to shut it off automatically is frayed. Give me your hand—I'll show you." He grabbed Maggie's hand and pulled it, lifting it up and running it along the plastic casing of a wire in the ceiling. "I think you made the right choice, by the way. That must've been hard."

"Yeah," Maggie shrugged. "It kind of was. I mean...my boyfriend didn't want it either, but I think that was for the best. He would have made a crappy dad."

Rob lowered himself to his regular, still-tall height and fixed Maggie with that quiet look again. "What a jerk."

"I'll live," Maggie gave his hand a squeeze and he let go. "Do you like cookies?"

They decided to sit on the street curb and argue about politics. Well, Maggie argued. Rob sat beside her and shook his head, or shrugged noncommittally as he chomped down on the semi-homemade chocolate chip creations that Maggie had produced from her mini-fridge.

"Now," Maggie said as she pushed the last cookie towards him. "Sam has great faith in the bureaucratic system. I keep telling him that the entire thing is so convoluted that there's no way it's actually functioning—my old history teacher used to say that it was all a big ponzi scheme and that one day it would all fall down around our ears before anyone knew what was happening. What do you think?"

"I think you need to get some new books," Rob said. "A U.S. History textbook isn't exactly light reading. I think my sister has some of those old whatchamacallems...Hark? Harley?"

"Harlequins? Harlequin romances?" Maggie grinned. "Those are right up my alley. I'm not really into the sexy ones, though. Betty Neels and Barbara Cartland are the ones for me."

"Cartland's the one who always writes the damsels in distress, right?"

"Yep. They're always saved in the end by a rogue-turned-gentleman. It's great. There's all sorts of things—duels, highway robbery, attempted murder, heaving bosoms..."

"Maybe I should give those a try."

"You're just in it for the bosoms."

"Hey!" Rob gave Maggie a gentle nudge. "I happen to be a very intellectually...sound...guy."

"Say that again when you've actually finished a Cartland."

"Maybe I will," he shrugged. "I could bring you some too...if you want."

Maggie gasped and slapped Rob's shoulder. "Seriously? You'd do that?"

"Well..." he cleared his throat. "I mean, yeah. If you like 'em so much."

"That would be fantastic!" she curled her fingers around her baby bump and tapped out a soft rhythm. "The romance novels at the gas station never hold the same appeal for me."

"Wait," Rob sighed. "Don't tell me you've been walking back and fort from this place to do shopping *and* work."

Maggie shrugged. "The bus is too expensive. I'm trying to save up so I have enough money to buy Maggie Junior some clothes and stuff when the time comes. Besides, it's not too far."

"Mags, come on. You're having a baby."

"Exercise is important for expectant moms," she raised her eyebrows. "Everybody says."

"Listen," Rob leaned back on his hands. "Just tell me whenever you need to shop or go somewhere and I'll give you a ride."

"I can't do that."

"Why not?"

"You already drive me to work. I can't start treating you like you're my own personal chauffeur."

"It's better than you wandering around town alone."

"It's not like I'm in danger. I can protect myself."

"I'm sure you can," Rob took a deep breath. "But it would make me...*feel* better knowing that you're not lying dead in a ditch somewhere."

"Aw," Maggie hummed and knocked against his shoulder with her own. "You like me!"

"What?" Rob snapped, and scooted away from her. "I never said that. Who said that?"

"You did! Well, not in so many words, but you worried about me, which means that we're at least sort-of friends, right?" Maggie tugged at the sleeve of his shirt and either didn't notice, or chose to ignore the excited shudder that contorted Rob's face.

"Uh," he cleared his throat. "Yeah. Friends."

"Woohoo!" Maggie kicked her feet out and leaned back on the sidewalk to mirror his pose. "Look at us. Two buddies. Pals...bros...homies..."

"Please, never say that word again."

"What?"

"You know what."

"'Homie' happens to be a perfectly good slang word. Embrace it, Robbie. Embrace the English language."

That night, after Rob had made her promise three separate times that she would wait for him to come pick her up for work, and after he had roared off in his pickup truck, Maggie dressed for bed and couldn't help smiling at her reflection in the mirror as she brushed her teeth.

The next weekend, after a brief talk with Sam asking if he could line up their days off with one another—a request that he agreed too with a knowing wink and a pointed nudge against Rob's ribs—the pair made a trip to the local bulk grocery store. One look at the inside of Maggie's fridge and Rob's mind had been made up—microwave pasta and frozen blackberry puree was no way for a pregnant woman to eat.

"Okay," he said, motioning for her to get a cart to mirror his. "I've got a list."

Maggie rolled her eyes. "You made a list for *my* shopping."

"Yeah," he made a fist and held it up, ticking off items on each finger as he spoke. "Greens, *fresh* fruit and veg, grains, protein..."

"Yuck," Maggie placed her hands protectively over her stomach. "Don't listen to the mean man, baby!"

Rob let go of his cart, ignoring it as it coasted forward and wedged itself against a stack of crates. "Ignore your mom, kiddo. I'm the one with your best interests at heart."

"Wow. Rude!"

By the end of their march through the store, both carts were brimming with items—not all food. Rob had made sure to fulfill every requirement on his list, much to Maggie's chagrin, but he also kept an eye out for other helpful things.

"A back scratcher?" she frowned at him.

"Everyone has to scratch their back," Rob shrugged. "I'd rather you didn't break your water while you try to hit yours."

She turned up her nose. "That's disgusting. Besides, my back doesn't itch."

"Next we're getting you vitamins."

"I already have food. Why do I need those?"

"And one of those 'What to Expect' books, because you're scaring me a little bit, Mags."

"You do realize that I can't afford half this crap, right? We're going to have to put it all back before we leave."

"You're not the one buying, so…"

"What?" With a spurt of strength, Maggie crashed her cart into his, bringing him to a halt mid-glide. "You are *not*."

"Try and stop me, babe."

"Babe? What, are you trying to sweet talk me?" Maggie raised her eyebrows threateningly. She'd decided that morning that real pants were too much trouble to put on, so she'd opted for baggy sweatpants, an 'I'm with stupid' tee shirt and an ancient hoodie; her long brown hair bobbed on top of her head in a precarious knot. The effect was far less intimidating than she had meant it to be, but it still made Rob want to take a step back. "You're not going to buy food for me to eat. You already fixed my A/C. It's not right."

"Hey," Rob held up both his hands in the universal signal of surrender. "I'm just trying to help you out here."

"Help?" Maggie brushed a loose strand of hair out of her face. "Help? I don't ne—need help, Rob. I can do this all on my own." Her eyes filled with tears, and her bottom lip began to tremble.

"Uh-oh," Rob muttered, and reached out to pat her shoulder. "Slow down. I never said you couldn't do it by yourself."

"You're trying to buy hundreds of d-dollars of stuff for me," Maggie wailed, "because I need help!"

Rob slid an arm around her shoulders and pulled her to the side, away from the foot traffic. "Yeah, I did, because I'm trying to show you that I'm a nice guy. Okay? Not because I think you're weak or out of your depth or…whatever. I want to help you. Not because I don't think you can handle it, but because I want you to know I'm your friend. I'm here. Got it?"

"I already know you're my friend, though." Maggie pulled a sleeve over her wrist and wiped at her watery eyes.

"Yeah," Rob winced. "I know you do."

"How about we split it? I pay for half, you pay for half."

"Sixty-forty."

"Fifty-fifty or I don't buy *anything*."

Rob leaned his head back and groaned. "You're so mean to me, Mags."

"You're too nice to me, Robbie."

They pushed their carts, side by side, to the checkout, and nodded placatingly when the checkout lady asked the 'happy couple' when they were due. They were taking turns riding their carts across the parking lot, earning dirty looks from the other customers, when someone called Maggie's name.

"Yeah?" she laughed in answer, stepping off of the cart's lower shelf and turning around. Rob watched the smile freeze on her face and pulled his cart back so that he was standing in front of her by a few inches before he turned as well.

It was a group of kids, about Maggie's age—five or six of them, mostly girls and one or two boys.

"Oh my God!" one of the girls, a smallish blonde, squealed and lunged past Rob before he could do anything, flinging her arms around Maggie's torso in a death grip. "Oh my God!"

"We couldn't believe it was you!" another exclaimed. "Maggie Hendricks. Alive and *shopping*!"

Maggie pried the girl's arms off of her. "Careful," she said. "Don't hurt her."

The blonde gasped. "Right!" she squeaked. "The baby. Oh my God, the baby. Can I touch?"

Maggie sighed. "Yeah." She glanced over at Rob and shrugged. "Friends from school," she mouthed. He nodded, but didn't stand down.

"We saw your parents at church last week," the blonde said as she caressed Maggie's stomach. "They asked about you—asked if we'd heard from you."

"Why didn't you call us?" one of the other girls—a taller redhead—asked. She was frowning. "We've been so worried about you. We *missed* you."

"John broke that bastard's nose, by the way," the blonde said, pointing to the boy in their group. "He transferred out after, you know, the thing you two had in the lunch room? What a loser."

"Yeah," Maggie said, a hesitant smile. "He really was."

"And who's this guy?" the blonde finally turned her attention towards Rob. "He bothering you?"

"Yeah," John stepped forward. "What's your name?"

"Guys," Maggie stepped in front of Rob. "This is Rob. We work together. He's my...friend."

"Huh." The redhead's eyes narrowed. "Friend, huh?"

"Yeah. He's cool, trust me." Maggie turned and winked at him. "Listen, we've got to go—he's got an early morning shift, and I'm craving some DQ like *crazy* if you know what I mean. But, uh...email me or something. I missed you guys."

"Oh," the girls in the group converged on Maggie in a mass hug. Cries of "We missed you more," or "never do that to us again," or "we thought you were dead," filled the air.

"They're going to tell my parents where they saw me," Maggie said on the way back to her apartment. "Two of those girls were in my youth group."

"I can't imagine you in a youth group," Rob chuckled. "Like, bible study and that stuff? Wow."

"I liked it," Maggie shrugged. "I was all into that sort of stuff. Service, crafts, summer camp. You know." She glanced down at her baby bump.

"I was too, actually. For a while," Rob shrugged. "More boy scout stuff, I guess. But...you know, my dad died, mom lost her job."

"You had to work?"

"Oh yeah. Finished high school and then I was off to the nearest garage, changing oil, wiping up after...it paid the bills, but it kind of sucked, so I did some other...not good stuff that I liked better for a couple years."

"Is that how you got the tattoo? Doing 'not good stuff'?"

"You been wanting to ask that question for a while?" Rob laughed. "Yeah. I got it then—I thought it'd make me look intimidating, but I guess it just comes off as punk."

"I dunno," Maggie shook her head. "It's kind of hot, actually."

Rob inhaled too quickly and hacked into his sleeve. "Thanks...?"

"You want to help me put stuff away? I slid some ice cream in there at the end."

Rob agreed, and accepted that by 'help' she meant 'put everything away for me.'

Afterward, they sat outside on the curb again, ice cream cones in hand, and watched as the sun set and cars whizzed past.

"I think I should call my parents," Maggie said, and licked her cone free of a stray drip. "I mean...what they wanted me to do wasn't fair, but I don't want them to worry..."

"If you feel like it's right, do it," Rob nodded. "Just don't let them do anything you don't want to do."

"I won't. I think...I think I'm strong enough to say no now. Instead of running away, I mean."

"Good." Rob bit down on his ice cream and shivered.

"I don't want to go home, though." Maggie frowned. "I'm happy here. With you." Her hand brushed his.

"So am I," Rob reached out and caught her fingers in his. "So am I, Mags."

The rest of the week was business as usual—he picked her up in the morning, they exchanged funny looks while she waited tables or dried his dishes, and then they held hands when he drove her home.

Then, she called him.

Saturday morning, as he lay tangled in his small bed, in an apartment hardly bigger than Sam's kitchen, his phone began to vibrate against the cheap tin nightstand.

"Hello," he said when he answered, and let his head fall back onto the soft pillow that he had been trying to settle back into only moments before.

"Rob?" Maggie squeaked. "I did it."

Rob's eyes flew open. "What?" he asked. "Did what?"

"I called my parents. And told them where I am. And they want to come *get me*."

"What, take you home for the weekend or something? That's great."

"No. They want to take me back to live with them. I tried to explain but they wouldn't listen to me, Rob."

"Are you home?" He sat up and reached for the jeans that he'd worn the day before. "Wait for me. I'm on my way." And hung up.

Later, Rob would swear up and down that traffic had been heavier than on regular weekdays. He beat a terrified staccato rhythm against the wheel at every stop light and gritted his teeth as he roared through the streets.

They were there—Maggie's parents—when he pulled up to the curb. They were an older couple, with graying hair and conservative semi-casual-Friday wear. Rob didn't even bother to pull his keys out of the ignition.

"Mags," he called, bypassing the couple and stepping down into the stairwell. The door was shut.

"Young man," her mother hissed. "What do you think you're doing?"

"Who do you think you are?" her father growled. "And how do you know our daughter?"

"Back off," Rob snapped, and tapped against the door. "Mags, it's me. Open up."

The blinds of her small window flipped open and shut. The door cracked.

"Hi," she said, and gave him a thin-lipped smile. "Do they look mad?"

"Margaret," her mother called. "Is that you?"

"No," Rob lied. "Come on out and explain. You can do this, remember?"

"Yeah," Maggie breathed. "You'll stick around?"

"Wouldn't miss this for the world."

"Okay. Let me take the chain off." The door shut again.

"Where did she go?" Maggie's father barked. "What did you say to her? I have my lawyer on speed dial."

The door opened fully, and Maggie saw Rob mid-eye roll.

"They're not that bad," she said.

"He wants to sue me and he doesn't even know my name."

"Daddy," Maggie placed one hand on Rob's chest and pushed him back so that she could step out into the stairwell. "Rob's a nice guy. I called him over here."

"You *called* him?" Maggie's mom gasped. "Honey, he has a *tattoo*."

"Yeah, he does," Maggie said slowly, as though she was explaining something very complicated. "And I think it's great. He's been taking good care of me for the last little while."

Rob grinned.

"I'm sure he has," her father said slowly. "I'm sure he has, honey, but...it's time for you to come home and let us take care of you the way we wanted to."

"She knows how you wanted to take care of her," Rob growled and nudged Maggie behind him. "And she's not going anywhere unless she gives the say-so."

"What's he talking about, sweetie?" Maggie's mom leaned over the stairs. "Take care of what?"

"I heard you talking," Maggie squeaked from behind Rob. Her hand tugged at his sleeve. "About what to do with the baby. You know. So I...I left."

"You heard..." Maggie's father's brow furrowed, and then his eyes widened. "Oh, Martha, she means..."

"Maggie," the mom gasped. "We weren't seriously...we were talking about what options we had, we *never* even *considered* that."

"You didn't?" Rob glared up at them.

"Oh no," Maggie's mother shook her head and clasped a hand over her slack jaw. "Oh no, we could never...we knew how you felt about it."

"You did?" Maggie peeked out from behind Rob. "You swear?"

"Yes!" Maggie's father yelled. "We swear. Please, Margaret...we've been so worried."

"Oh, dad." Maggie's hand slid down to give Rob's a squeeze before she pushed past him and rushed up the stairs to wrap her arms around her father's neck. "I missed you guys."

"You'll come home, then?" Her mother sighed. "Oh, we're so happy..."

"Well..." Maggie sighed and kissed her mother's cheek. "Not...exactly." She glanced back at Rob.

"Oh," her mom said. "Oh, I see."

"See what?" Maggie's father asked from where his face was pressed into his daughter's neck. "What's happening?"

"Our girl's found herself a *friend*, David." Martha's eyes flicked over to Rob. "And judging by the way he was snapping over her just now, I'd say he feels the same way. Right, young man?"

"It's Rob, mom." Maggie glanced over her shoulder. "I mean...we haven't dated. He doesn't..."

"Yes we have," Rob almost shouted. "I fixed your air conditioning and we went shopping, which technically counts as dinner..."

"Ooh!" Maggie screeched, pushing her father away. "Ooh! You like me back?"

"Like you," he said as he stepped up the stairs and slid an arm around her rounded waist. "Love you *both*. Whatever."

He looked down at her upturned face and pressed his lips to her forehead. "We're a family."

"You know what?" she said, her smile widening. "I think we are."

LET ME CALL YOU SWEETHEART

CHELSEA COTTON

42

Jack met Maryanne in a bar. It wasn't the best love story from the sounds of it, but it wasn't a normal bar either. It was 1963, and that was where all of the local twenty-somethings went to dance.

Jack had just gotten back from a tour of duty. He wore his military uniform to the bar. He sat at one of the high tops and ordered a beer.

"Do you want to dance?" He heard behind him, as he brought the bottle to his lips.

He turned around and saw her there: purple dress with white polka dots, blonde hair sculpted perfectly to flip at her shoulders . . . Jack almost spit out his beer right there.

"Are you asking me to?" he asked.

"Well, I like to give a man in uniform a little fun," she flirted.

Jack set down his beer. "Do you say that to every man you see in a uniform?"

"Only the cute ones," she admitted.

"Oh," he laughed. "So I'm cute. Well my, my you have a way with words, little lady. What's your name?"

She smiled. "Maryanne."

The two of them danced that night, and every night of the week for a month. Eventually they fell in love, and, as fate would have it, Jack married Debbie, the girl he grew up next door to.

Fifty years later, Jack was sitting on the bed, with his dear Debbie standing in front of him, a shoebox in her hand.

"I was looking for your dress shoes," she said, hysterical. "For the funeral. You know, Ken's funeral. My brother. My best friend. The man who said I shouldn't marry you because you were the type of child that would push people off their bicycles. Well, I found these instead. You know what these are, Jack? Do you?"

He did. He debated playing stupid or not. He never knew exactly what type of mood Debbie was in.

"They're LOVE LETTERS!" She threw the shoebox at him, narrowly missing his head. "LOVE LETTER TO MARYANNE!

They're years old. Years! And you still have them?! What, did you want to start a shrine or something? DID YOU JACK?!"

Jack didn't say anything.

Debbie huffed and puffed, and before the argument escalated further, the two of them heard the front door open and a voice call out, "Hey Ma! Hey Dad!"

Jack groaned. Debbie shot him a nasty look, before going out to the kitchen. Jack looked at the love letters, that had fallen out of the shoebox and sprinkled out onto the bed, before sighing and following his wife out to the kitchen.

"Hey, Dad," Carol said, assuming her usual spot looking in the fridge. She pulled out a block of cheese. "Don't give Gavin, this, okay? He had diarrhea for a week."

Gavin, Carol's only sheltered child, was practically wrapped around his mother's legs. He was ten, with glasses and slightly greasy hair.

"Hey, kid," Jack said.

"Kids are goats, Dad." Carol rolled her eyes, pulled and apple out of the fridge, crossed the room to wash it in the sink and handed it to Gavin.

"Back in my day he would have eaten that right off the tree," Jack joked.

"I don't want my child to get poisoned by pesticides." Carol rolled her eyes.

Debbie walked in the room at that moment, and hugged her daughter and grandson. As they exchanged their hellos, Jack noticed that he wife did not acknowledge him and slowly withered in guilt upon her finding the letters. It was just something she wasn't going to understand, and he did not know how to explain it.

Carol finally left, and Debbie retreated to the dining room table to clip some coupons, leaving Jack alone with Gavin. Jack wanted nothing more than to head down to the basement and watch TV, but there was no way a kid like Gavin would be okay with that. Carol never let him watch TV, and for some reason Gavin believed that his brain would turn to mush if he did.

Instead, the two of them played a game of chess in the living room. Neither of them were very good chess players, which made the game pretty boring. Jack attempted small talk with his only grandson.

"So . . . how's school?"

"Good." Jack shrugged.

"What school is it again . . . a moon sore . . .?"

"Montessori," Gavin said, capturing Jack's knight with his bishop. "We're learning how to knit."

"Isn't that a little girly?" Jack asked.

Gavin smiled. "Mom told me you might say that if I told you."

Jack moved a pawn, and instantly was scooped up by Gavin's rook. "Do you have a girlfriend?"

"Grandpa," Gavin groaned. "I'm only ten."

"Right."

They finished their chess game, Jack losing gloriously, and then continued another one. Halfway through, Jack scooted away to use the restroom, purposely taking a little longer than usual to wash his hands. When he went back into the living room, he discovered Gavin was gone, and the door to the bedroom was open slightly.

Jack peeked into the room, to see Gavin sitting on the bed, looking at the letters sprinkled everywhere.

"Gavin . . ." Jack began.

"Who's Maryanne?" Gavin asked.

"Your grandmother," Jack lied.

"Grandma's name is Debra," Gavin said. "But nice try."

Jack sighed. There were some conversations he never planned on having with his grandson, and this was one of them. This was a conversation he had never planned to have period, however his snooping wife made that very difficult. Yet, for some reason, maybe it was because Gavin was the product of Carol, he felt as though he had to explain himself.

He sat on the bed next to his grandson, and said, "Those are letters to my ex girlfriend."

"Why are you writing letters to your ex girlfriend?" Gavin asked.

"Those are old."

"Why didn't you send them?"

It was a moment where Jack debated telling Gavin the truth, but then again not even Debbie knew the truth, and although the kid was adorable there was a good chance he would tell his mother what his grandfather had told him. "It's complicated."

"Why did you keep them?"

Jack sighed. "That's even more complicated.

Gavin bit his lip, and pushed his glasses up to prevent them from slipping down the edge of his nose. "You know how you asked me earlier if I had a girlfriend?"

"Yeah," Jack said, confused about the abrupt subject change, yet not at all hesitant about letting it move forward.

"Well." Gavin pushed his glasses again. "There is a girl I like. But I don't think she would even notice me."

"What's her name?" Jack asked.

"Hazel." Gavin blushed. "She's in my class. We sit next to each other and when we were knitting last week she showed me how to use a cable hook. She even touched my hand and . . . I felt butterflies and stuff."

Gavin was bright red. Jack tried not to laugh at the ridiculous sight, or even more so that the two little lovebirds bonded over knitting. "Well," he said. "Do you talk to her?"

"Sometimes." Gavin shrugged. "But lately I just get tongue tied."

"Tell her," Jack said. "Next time you see her laugh . . ." For a moment, he thought of her. "That her eyes sparkle when she does."

Jack met Debbie when they were four. Debbie's family moved next door to him. With an alcoholic father and a tired mother, Jack found himself at Debbie's house a lot, hanging out with her brother Hank who was only a year older than them. Jack and Hank formed a tight friendship, one that lasted after Jack married his little sister.

That afternoon after Carol picked up Gavin, Jack could feel the ice coming off of Debbie. The second he walked into the dining room and saw her clipping coupons, he could feel it, and his bones were so cold they were going to snap.

"Hey," he said.

"Don't." She held up her hand. "I am so done with hearing excuses from you. I don't know why you're writing to her, more importantly I don't know why you're stupid enough to make copies of the letters, but that is besides the point."

"You realize I didn't make copies," Jack said. "You realize those are originals. I never sent them to her. She wouldn't get them anyway."

"But you still wrote them." Debbie looked up, and Jack felt like her eyes were going to slice him in half. "You wrote them and I read them and there they are. You couldn't throw them away, you just hung onto them for years to come. So congratulations. I'm hurt, and you're a pig. Just go away."

Defeated, Jack decided to do what Debbie told him to do, so he retreated to the local bar to meet Hank. The two ordered beers and meatball subs, and watched the football game on the TV.

"Debbie found my Maryanne letters," Jack admitted around half time.

Hank was a very protective older brother, but he was also a very over protective best friend, making him a good buffer for either Jack or Debbie whenever they fought. "How did that go?" he asked.

"Not good," Jack said. He finished his beer, and acknowledged the bar tender to bring him another one. "She's mad at me, giving me the cold shoulder. Gavin was over today and she wouldn't even hide it from him."

"How is the brat?"

"That's a strong word," Jack said. "He's not so much bratty as sheltered. I gotta tell ya, I knew Carol wasn't the happiest kid, but her mother and I gave her a good childhood. I don't know why she feels the need to baby that kid."

"She had a kid a little weird too," Hank says. "That donor thing she did."

"Who could stand being around her," Jack joked, and then felt bad. It was his daughter after all.

"So . . . what are you going to do about Debbie?" Hank asked, bringing it back on subject. "I mean, she doesn't really know the truth about what happened between the two of you. Can't blame her for being ignorant."

Jack saw truth in Hank's statement, but he still did not know what to do.

When he got home, Jack found his wife in the living room, laying on the couch reading a book.

"What are you reading?" he asked.

"A book," she replied.

"Descriptive." Jack was getting annoyed with Debbie's behavior. When she found the letters he expected her to be a little upset, and yell at him, but he wasn't expecting this type of treatment.

She did not bother to look up at him. Jack even noticed that she was still dressed, which was odd because usually she would get into her pajamas before her nightly read. He waited for her to maybe say something to him, but she didn't. He decided to leave, but before he could, she asked, "How was the bar?"

"I met Hank," he replied. "We had dinner together. He's doing well. Lily's back from college and moving in with the boyfriend, so that makes him and Betsy crazy. You know these kids now a days, they think they could just move in with the first person they think they fall in love with and all will be dandy. I'm glad neither of our kids did that."

"And Maryanne? Was she there too?"

Jack sucked in his breath. "No," he said, firmly. "I watched the game with your brother, and we had beer and subs and talked about how much I love you."

Without another word, Jack headed to bed. When Debbie finally joined him, she made it a point to face away from her husband the entire night.

School was canceled again for Gavin the next day, so Carol dropped him off, and washed him an apple.

"Gavin tells me they're learning to knit in class," Jack said.

"Yep, Dad." Carol sighed, and handed Gavin the apple. "They are.

"Don't you think there is something more useful he could learn?" Jack shrugged. "Like algebra. I don't get why you're paying this much money for a private school that doesn't even teach him things he needs to know."

"When is he going to use algebra?" Carol asked.

"When is he going to need knitting."

Carol rolled her eyes, and then gave Gavin a kiss on the top of the head. "Love you, sweetie. Call me if Grandpa gets all crazy on you."

"I will."

Carol hugged Debbie, who had dipped inside the kitchen to say hello to her daughter. The two of them were close; and Jack suspected it was because Debbie never gave Carol crap for her weird parenting choices. Then again, Jack also suspected that Debbie might have been a little scared of Carol. Their daughter was a bit of a terrifying human being.

Jack hoped that Debbie would join him and Gavin so we wouldn't be stuck hanging out together. Jack even dared to maybe think that Debbie would take over Kid Duty so he could go and watch TV in the basement and maybe take a nap. However, that apparently was not going to happen. Once again, Debbie went to the dining room to clip coupons, and Gavin and Jack were playing chess.

"How have thinks been going with Grandma?" Gavin asked, as he began to beat his grandfather.

"Horrible," Jack admitted. His head wasn't focused in the game. "How have things been going with Hazel?"

"I haven't seen her since yesterday," Gavin said, rolling his eyes. "I was thinking of maybe writing her a letter."

"Don't let another girl see it," Jack warned. "That could lead to trouble."

Gavin smiled. "I won't. Hazel is the love of my life, Grandpa."

Even though he was ten, Jack found Gavin's statement to be positively adorable. He even choked up a little. He grabbed a piece of paper and a pen from the basement, and together him and Gavin sat on the floor to create the letter for Hazel.

"Dear Hazel . . ." Gavin started.

"Darling Hazel," Jack said. "That's better."
"Darling Hazel." Gavin bit his lip. "Now what?"

"Darling Hazel . . ." Jack thought of the love of his life, and the time when he once had to learn how to woo her with words. "Darling . . . I remember the first time I ever saw you."

"I don't though," Gavin said. "We were in kindergarten. She wasn't even a person to me then."

"You never tell a woman that," Jack warned. "You always want to make them feel like they have been special to you since the day you met."

Gavin nodded. "Darling Hazel . . . I remember the first time I ever saw you. We were in kindergarten and you were wearing your hair in two braids."

"That's good." Jack nodded. "Now say why you remember that."

Gavin nodded again, a little smile curling on his lips. "You said hi to me when no one else did and you became my friend."

"That sounds a little pathetic," Jack said. "She doesn't want to hear about how she's your only friend and no one else would talk to you."

"But it's the truth."

"Yeah, but you don't tell her that."

"Well, what should I say?"

Jack thought for a moment. "You said hi to me, and in that moment I felt warm in my heart and knew we were meant to be friends."

"I didn't feel warm in my heart," Gavin said. "We were five."

"Don't mention that part."

"There's a lot of things we aren't supposed to mention," Gavin said, but he did not seem frustrated, more like excited.

After about an hour, the letter to Hazel was perfectly crafted:

Darling Hazel,

I remember the first time I ever saw you. You said hi to me, and in that moment I felt warm in my heart and knew we were meant to be friends. Now that we are older, I feel as though it is time to tell you just how much you mean to me. I am in love with you. I am in love with your beauty and your grace. You complete me. You're like a character out of a Shakespearean sonnet. We are better than Romeo and Juliet because we are not complete morons that would disappoint our parents and actually speak like normal human beings. Hazel, every day with you is a blessing, and I hope that those days will last of all eternity. Even if for some reason we have to be in different classes next year, I will always make it work with you, if you would do me the honor of letting me into your life and into your heart. I love you, Hazel. Will you be my Valentine this year, and every year?

Love always,

Gavin

It was the perfect letter, and when Carol came to pick Gavin up, Jack gave him a wink goodbye. He heard his grandson tell his mother how much fun he had with his grandfather and, satisfied and optimistic, Jack turned towards his wife. She was at the sink, pretending to wash the few dishes left over from when the other two had lunch, staring out the window in frustration.

"My darling Debra," he said.

"Don't you mean *Maryanne*." Without any hesitation, Debbie dropped the plate she was holding into the soapy water and walked out of the kitchen to somewhere in the house, leaving her husband far behind.

Jack was heartbroken, so that night he decided to go for a drive and think about the first date he ever went on with Debbie. It was an Italian bistro, known for good wine and even better chicken parm. Jack had bought her flowers, a bouquet of yellow roses because Hank had told him those were her favorite. He wore a blue tie because when he was younger he remembered her saying that her favorite article of clothing on a man was a blue tie. He wore expensive cologne that he only broke out for special occasions. He gelled his hair. He brushed his teeth five times to make sure they were more than clean. And he spent the entire night whispering nothing but sweet words to her, and everything he said was absolutely and positively true. Jack spoiled Debbie that night, like he had never spoiled a woman before. Not even Maryanne.

The latter had always told him how to spoil a woman. "Remember," she said, as one of the last things she ever said to someone. "Remember to always spoil your future wife."

"Why can't you be my future wife?" he asked her.

"You know why, Jack."

"I don't know why."

"You know why."

Jack found himself near the graveyard, and he decided since he was he was going to visit his parents. He parked outside the gate, and when he went to their graves he sat down, ignoring the popping sound coming from his knees. His mother had died just a few years before, his father a year before that. The two of them loved Maryanne. The two of them also loved Debbie.

He thought about their love story; how his father was a WWII Vet and his mother was a factory worker. He thought about how they raised three boys and a girl, all the meanwhile maintaining a loving relationship. He had wished to have that with Debbie. And they did at first. They got married, a year later had Carol, and two years after that her brother Paul. When the kids left, Jack still loved Debbie, and when Gavin came along, Jack still loved Debbie. But he began to worry that Debbie did not love him. As awful as it sounded, Jack began to think of a different life; a life that did not include Debbie, that instead was swapped with Maryanne.

He always felt guilty about what happened with Maryanne, even though it was not his fault, or so everyone convinced him it wasn't. Deep down, Jack did understand that. He had no way to defeat science and did not have any control over Maryanne and whatever happened to her. Sometimes, though, he looked at every activity they did together and wondered whether or not that could have attributed to her decline.

"What do I do?" he asked his parents, as though he were a child again, and as though maybe just maybe they had any such idea of how to answer his question.

Alas, the dead did not give any answers.

When Jack got home, he found Debbie already asleep. He went down to the basement to watch TV, ultimately falling asleep there. He secretly hoped when he woke up the next morning for Gavin to be coming over, but the morning news channel did not report any school cancellations. However, that did mean that Gavin would be given the chance to give Hazel his letter. Jack looked forward to hearing about it. Even the weird ones needed to find love sometimes.

Debbie wasn't up yet, so he decided to make her breakfast. When they had first gotten married, he made her breakfast every morning. They honey mooned in a little cottage on the coast of Maine. He woke up every morning and made her breakfast every day they were on their honey moon. He would bring it to her in bed, alongside a seashell he picked off the beach and a handwritten note.

He broke out the pancake mix and a banana and chocolate chips. He stirred the batter and followed the directions carefully. Sometimes he liked to be inventive with his cooking, and since it usually went disastrous it drove Debbie absolutely crazy. As he poured the batter into the skillet, he made coffee and laid out her cup with sugar and creamer so that he could pour the coffee right it. Right as he was flipping the last batch of pancakes, his wife walked into the kitchen, already fully dressed for the day, not in her usual bathrobe that she wore whenever she ate breakfast.

"Morning," Jack greeted her, smiling a little too enthusiastically. "I made you pancakes."

"I'm on a diet."

Debbie helped herself to an apple out of the fridge, washed it like Carol always did for Gavin, and then grabbed a cup of coffee, and then left the room, leaving Jack alone with his chocolate chip banana pancakes. He could feel the disappointment bubbling up inside him, but instead of being frustrated he felt himself getting very sad.

He ate a few pancakes alongside of a class of orange juice and cup of coffee, and wrapped the others up to put in the fridge. He knew his wife. She would sneak a couple when he wasn't looking, and when he caught her the two of them would laugh over the whole thing and pretend as though the past few days and their animosity towards each other had never happened.

Jack spent the day in his recliner, because honestly he did not know what else to do besides bother Debbie and make her even more upset. He watched a couple soap operas, and reruns of *Survivor.* He took a nap. He picked his finger nails. He heard the garage door open a few times, listening to when Debbie was leaving and coming to do her errands.

Jack almost missed Gavin, even though the kid was a bit weird. He had fun constructing the letter to Hazel with him, as well as getting beat in chess. He debated whether or not to call the kid, but then remembered he was in the weird school his mother sent him too. Jack debated calling Carol, but Debbie was already giving him enough of a headache. He didn't need Carol to give him one too.

Jack read the news paper, and then took a little nap, and when he woke up he watched some more TV. He heard the garage door open again, and the car parked, and Debbie walked inside. He debated going up to greet her and offer to make her lunch, but what was the point?

Around three o'clock the phone rang. When he saw Carol's number on the caller ID, he smiled in excitement. "Gavin!" he answered. "How are ya, kid?"

"No, Dad." It was Carol. She sounded mad. "What made you think it was appropriate to teach my son how to write a love letter?"

"What?" Jack decided to play dumb.

"Gavin showed me the letter you wanted him to give to Hazel." Carol was really mad. Jack could hear it. It almost sounded like she was screaming.

"Why would he show you that?" Jack was confused, and felt a little betrayed.

"He tells me everything, Dad. We don't have a relationship built on lies and mistrust. Gavin also told me that he found your letters to your ex girlfriend and that started this little experiment. Nice."

"It was a letter to a girl he liked!" Jack defended himself. He wasn't even going to mention anything about Maryanne. "It was supposed to be cute! Come on, it's not like he was writing anything sexual to the girl. You're being way too over protective, Carol, I never helicoptered over you like you do to him and you turned out fine. Lighten up!"

"He shouldn't be telling a girl he loves her, he's ten!" Carol groaned. "Honestly, Dad, it's like you never even raised a kid. What were you thinking?!"

"You're not raising a kid, he's a human!" Jack barked.

"You're so frustrating!" Jack could almost see Carol pulling her hair. "SO frustrating! You're not his parent, this was *totally* not appropriate, and don't use my son as a tool to get back at Mom. YOU messed up, YOU fix it. Don't get my fifth grader involved!"

With that, Jack heard the phone slam, and he actually felt a little guilty.

The first time they kissed, it was in a bookstore. They were walking down the aisles, grabbing books and reading the first sentence, playing a game in which they were deciding whether or not the book was good. Finally, Jack couldn't take it anymore, and he kissed her, deeply, like he had never kissed a woman before.

Maryanne smiled, and when she backed away she ran her fingers through her hair.

"You're going to kiss your wife like that, aren't you?"

"Why are you playing this up so much?" Jack asked. "Why are you so convinced you're not going to be my wife? That you're not going to live for a hundred years?"

"That would require a miracle," Maryanne said, and as she ran her fingers through her hair again, a piece of it fell out.

Finally, Jack was tired of Debbie's pouting. So much so that he stormed upstairs into the dining room, where his wife was reading a magazine.

"You're my wife," he demanded.

She looked up, startled at his anger. "Yes?"

"And I love you!" he exclaimed.

"Yes?" She raised her eyebrows.

"And . . ." He bit his lip and felt the tears well into his eyes. "I'm going to tell you what happened with me and Maryanne. And you're going to listen."

Jack and Debbie drove. She didn't say anything, and Jack thought maybe it was better that way. They drove for an hour, until they were outside of a large white building that Jack knew Debbie had never seen before. It was the last place that he ever imagined being again, but he had to go there. He had to explain to his wife why he had written all of those letters and that he never did anything to purposely hurt her. Jack parked in the parking lot and cut the ignition.

"Where are we?" Debbie asked. She was annoyed, Jack could tell.

"Newbury Medical Center." Jack pointed to the big red sign.

"Why?"

Jack knew this was the moment. He sighed, and felt his heart begin to race a little in agony. "This is the last place I saw Maryanne," he explained. He pointed to the left side of the building, that awkwardly jutted out from the rest in one single floor. "That is where I saw her. Right there. Inside."

"She dumped you in a hospital?"

"No." Jack shook his head. "She died."

On the day she left for good, Maryanne lay in her hospital bed. All of her hair had fallen out and she weighed no more than sixty pounds. Jack sat in a chair by her side.

"Promise me," his love said. "That you will kiss your wife the way you kissed me. That you will dance with her the way you danced with me. That you will love her no matter what."

"I can't promise that," Jack said, holding her hand, his body shaking in grief. "I cannot promise to love someone like that. I cannot because I will not."

"You're young," Maryanne said. "You're handsome. You're going to meet a woman and she's going to fall in love with you, and you're going to fall in love with her, and I need you to promise me that you will let her fall in love with you and you will let yourself love her the way you loved me."

"I can't," Jack said, as he began to cry.

"You will," Maryanne said. "You have to."

Later that night, after she had her final breaths, Jack met Hank at the bar. He cried and told him what happened, and the two of them drank. Hank invited Jack to a barbeque at his parents house the next day, if he felt up to it. They were celebrating that his sister Debbie was in town visiting, and that she said she would love to see Jack

Debbie and Jack sat in the car, and as Jack told her the story of Maryanne and the cancer and how they were only able to spend three months together, Debbie slowly began to understand what had been happening to her husband.

"I wrote them . . . to make sense of it all," Jack explained. "I did not write to Maryanne to tell her that I was still in love with her. I did not write to her to try and cheat on you. I am faithful to you, and Debra I love you more than anyone on this planet, but there was a time when I loved another woman and we were separated because of death. I will always cherish her, and when I am upset I turn to her to talk to because there are some things I just do not want to burden you with. But I love you Debbie, and I wish you would love me again too."

Debbie held her husband's hand. "Why did you tell me she dumped you?" she asked.

"Honestly?" He laughed a little. "Imagine if I had told you the day that I saw you again that my girlfriend had just died the night before, and then asked you if you wanted to go out with me. How do you think that would have turned out?"

"I would have thought you were crazy," Debbie said honestly, laughing.

"I loved you from the moment I saw you at that picnic in your parents' backyard," Jack explained. "But the timing was weird, and I panicked, and Maryanne always told me that whenever I met the woman I married to not do anything to turn her away."

"So . . ." Debbie said. "I have Maryanne to thank for you."

"You have you to thank for you," Jack said, then laughed. "Or whatever. That wording was weird, let's not lie. But Debra, I could never imagine my life without you. I could never imagine the world we built together just not existing. I could never imagine a world without you, or Carol or Paul or Gavin or even that girl that Paul is dating but is pretending not to date because he's scared we will embarrass him. I love everything that is you, and is us, and I would never change that for anything. You're my best friend, Debra. You're the absolute love of my life and I could never imagine my life without my best friend."

Debbie laughed softly, and she squeezed his hand tightly. She leaned over and gave Jack a kiss on the cheek, and then on the lips, and Jack felt that his wife was no longer an icicle freezing him out and that she had finally forgiven him. When she pulled away, Jack smiled. Sensing it was time, Jack turned over the ignition and began to drive home.

A week later, Carol stopped by with Gavin. While their daughter talked to her mother, their grandson went to see his grandfather in the basement.

"I'm sorry I told Mom about the letter," he said.

Jack didn't say anything. In truth, he had forgotten about the whole thing, but he thought it might be funnier if Gavin believed that he was still truly mad. So he sat in his chair, a frown on his face, noticing that Gavin was shaking like a leaf.

"Why did you?" Jack asked.

Gavin shrugged. "I thought maybe she would give me words of encouragement. She's my best friend she helps me feel better. But Grandpa . . . I have a secret."

"What is that?"

A mischievous smile appeared on Gavin's face. "I rewrote the letter and gave it to Hazel. She's my girlfriend now."

REACH FOR HIM

SARAH LOVE

Bridget Perry flipped down the visor against the afternoon sun as she steered in sweeping curves along the coastal road. She drew in her breath sharply. Her wrists hurt. She glanced at her wrists which were bruised and swollen and then averted her eyes. She didn't want to be reminded of them or of the event that caused them.

For the umpteenth time that day, tears welled in her eyes and spilled down her cheeks. Not even the stunning beauty of an Australian sunset could distract her from the heaviness in her heart. Images of her ex, came unbidden to her mind; his fathomless black eyes and raven hair falling long and wavy down his muscled back; his teeth white against swarthy skin. Bridget's breath caught in her throat. "Jackson," she whispered through her tears. She sighed one long shuddering miserable breath. Why was she crying over that two-timing, heartless pig anyway? Because I don't know how to be by myself, was the honest answer.

Bridget squinted and slowed down. With the sun at this angle she could barely see a few feet in front of her. She rounded the bend at a crawl and noticed a small motel sitting back away from the road, shrouded in thick foliage; a wooden sign peeped out from behind a heavy overhang of magenta flowers; Bougainvillea lodge it said in a cursive blue letters. Suddenly, Bridget wanted nothing more than to stop at here away from the sun, where she would be able to rest and recuperate. She pulled in and the gravel crunched in welcome as she parked the car. She stifled a groan. Sitting in the car for fourteen hours straight had done its work on her muscles. As she pulled herself out of the car and stretched her arms behind her head, she caught a glimpse of the view. Bougainvillea lodge had a perfect position facing the beach, which was, to her great relief, devoid of crowds, except for a lone walker and his dog and a young couple with small children paddling in the shallows.

The woman behind the counter welcomed her with just the right balance of warmth and respect for privacy that she needed, giving her a key and reminding her that dinner would be served at the restaurant at six. With slow deliberate steps, Bridget carried her bag, packed in such haste the night before and now she realized depressingly light, to her room. Not doubting that she had left most of her best clothes and belongings behind, she looked around the room. Nothing special, she thought, but adequate for her needs. The bathroom looked clean enough and turning back the bed, she was pleased to find crisp white cotton sheets. Right now that was all the mattered, a hot shower and sleep.

With her clothes strewn across the bathroom floor, she winced with pleasure as the hot water pummelled her tired and sore shoulders. She lathered up every part of her body and scrubbed. What she was scrubbing away she wasn't sure, but the need to be clean was overwhelming. There was more crying, but this time, the tears were more from relief than sadness. It felt good to be alone where no one could reach her or find her. She was so tired. It was all she could do to dry herself off and pull on some clean underwear and a t-shirt and crawl, exhausted into bed.

When she opened her eyes the room was dark with one brilliant shard of light spilling through a gap in the heavy drapes. Bridget reached out and felt her way over the bedside table for her phone. Her home screen glowed with a photo of Jackson during their holiday to Bali the year before. She frowned at it and focused on the time instead – 11.am! She flopped back on the pillows for a minute, amazed at how long she had slept. She lay there listening to her body. She felt relaxed and for the first time in ten months, safe.

Last April, Jackson had walked into her life and turned it upside down. He was mesmerizing in his masculine beauty. She was the envy of women wherever they went; she saw it in their eyes. Women, who ordinarily were shy and mousey, became predatory and catlike in his presence. He was talented, funny, and charming in public; but it hadn't taken long for her to realize that behind closed doors he was a cold, narcissistic bully. Ten months of verbal put-downs had left her believing that no other man would ever tolerate her the way he did. She had suspected cheating but had never been able to find any definitive evidence. He didn't need to cheat behind her back anyway. He was happy enough to flirt with other women right under her nose. On the rare occasion she called him out on it, he would jeer and tell her she was lucky to be with him and to leave if she didn't like it.

She didn't like it, but she didn't dare leave. Her best friend Nick had voiced his disapproval over and over. The image of him clenching his large, usually gentle, hands in frustration, came to mind. Dear, loyal Nick, with his lanky frame, round blue eyes, and freckled upturned nose, exactly the same as it had been when they played together as five-year-olds. He had always been there and she couldn't imagine the world without him in it. Some people winked and hinted that they would one day end up together, but she had always laughed at the idea. Nick was so safe. She knew him possibly better than she knew herself sometimes and she wanted mystery and adventure. As a result, her attention was too readily arrested by men who were exciting and unavailable in some way.

"It ticks me off," Nick had grumbled one day a few weeks into her relationship with Jackson. They were sitting on her couch watching re-runs of Seinfeld and eating chips.

"What ticks you off?"

"You, and other women too, always gushing slavishly over wankers like Jackass, I mean Jackson." He smiled wickedly. "What is it with women and bad boys? Do you actually want to be treated like crap?"

Bridget threw a cushion at Nick's head messing up the top of his straight brown hair. "He's not that bad!" She dodged the cushion on its return flight. "I don't know why but there's just something irresistible about a man who might not hang around. Knowing that he might go, but he's choosing to stay with me is sort of exciting, y'know?"

Nick's expression was incredulous. "No, I don't know! Bridge' that's the most ludicrous idea. The guy doesn't care about you! He puts you down! People don't do that to people they love, can't you see that?"

"He's had a rough life!" she countered. "His dad was a deadbeat. His mom had different men parading through his childhood. He didn't get shown much love and I want to make up for that. I think I can heal him if I love him enough."

Nick had stared at her long and hard, finally pulling her to him in a warm hug. "That isn't love Bridget. That's not how love works. Love isn't a one-way thing. It's like water." He pulled back and looked Bridget in the face. "Love is like water and people are like sponges. If you pour love into someone they should soak it up like a sponge, but if a person is like a rock, then the love just splashes and runs off the side getting wasted on the ground. Jackson's heart is a rock. You're wasting your love on him."

He had gone home after that and Bridget had thought about his analogy many times since then. It had all come to a head when last night after work, she had gone into their bathroom and found a woman's earring in the sink. She had confronted Jackson about it when he got home drunk in the early hours of the next morning, and instead of lying or being ashamed, he had mocked her and told her that the earring woman was here to stay and she could take it or leave it. She had screamed and thrown herself at him in a panicked rage and that was when he had grabbed her by the wrists twisting them cruelly and making her sink to the floor, a defeated wreck. She had packed a hurried bag and left there and then, not thinking or looking back and now 30 hours later she was here, alone, and finally free.

Pulling back the drapes of her motel room revealed a glorious Summer's day. From her window, the water glistened and the sand glowed white in the sun. It was much busier today. What had seemed like an empty country road the night before was now fringed with parked cars baking in the heat. Families strolled up and down and from the beach; the sounds of laughter and excited yelps carried across to her window.

Bridget threw on a pair of lavender shorts and a white cheesecloth peasant blouse. She looked at herself critically in the mirror. Her eyes still had a residue of puffiness from all the crying and over-sleeping but she didn't feel like wearing make-up. Her face stared back at her in solemn comradery. At 27, Bridget could still boast clear, olive skin with a smattering of freckles. Her best features apparently, were her large hazel eyes and long auburn hair. She curled her lip; obviously, Jackson didn't think they were that great. Before she could let her thoughts wander gloomily down that road, she pulled herself away from the mirror, grabbed her bag and left the room.

The air was balmy on her skin and the sound of her sandals slapping against the cool tiles brought a delicious sensation of Summer holidays bubbling up inside her. It seemed like the real Bridget was struggling up in revolt against the old, Jackson oppressed, Bridget, desperate to make a comeback. The lady behind the desk welcomed her with a smile.

"Nice day for it," she beamed. "Heading down to the beach?"

"Yep, just going for a stroll. It's busier than I expected it to be."

"That's because the agricultural show is on in Bluegum this week. When people get too hot traipsing around the showgrounds they inevitably end up here at Opal Bay to cool off. Are you going to the show today?"

Bridget let her mind wander for a moment. She imagined the showgrounds packed with hot sweaty people, crying children, loud music, and smelly livestock. She shook her head, smiling. "No, I think I'll just enjoy a peaceful day on the beach, thanks. How much are those straw hats?"

"That'll put you back ten dollars, love."

Bridget chose a broad-brimmed straw hat with a yellow and white polka-dot band. As she closed the door of the reception office behind her, she was hit with a wall of heat. In the scramble of departure, she hadn't thought to pack things like sunscreen. Without it, she was going to end the day red as a lobster, but throwing caution to the wind, she stepped out into the day with a 'come what may' attitude. She followed the sounds of laughter, seagulls, and surf across the road and through a scrubby pathway cut through the sand, slowing down against the resistance of the sand, panting a little at the effort. A couple of pre-teen boys hurtled past her, laughing like hyenas. They missed her by inches, covering her with sand in the process. She laughed out loud. She couldn't be angry. Their innocence was unapologetically refreshing.

An enticing aroma wafted over to her from a food stand that had been set up on the beach under a canopy. It was a sausage sizzle. Bridget's stomach growled; she hadn't given food a second thought since leaving Jackson, and now, all of a sudden, she felt that she could devour an entire side of beef. Two long lines of hungry beachgoers had formed at the stand, so Bridget took her place behind an elderly woman baked brown and wrinkled from a lifetime spent on Aussie beaches. Everyone was buying as much as they could in one go, and the line was moving slowly, so Bridget found herself watching the other people in the queue.

In the line next to her and a few places ahead, a tall person caught her eye. Bleached blond hair over a pair of broad tanned shoulders, tapering down to slim hips in turquoise board shorts made her smile in appreciation. She hoped he would turn around so that she could see his face. Come on, she urged mentally, turn around just a little bit. As if he heard her thoughts, the tall man turned and looked straight at her with startling blue eyes. He held her gaze just for a second and then turned back. Bridget felt like she had been hit by a sledgehammer. A very gorgeous, beach-babe kind of sledgehammer. "Just like Captain America," she murmured inwardly.

"You're too right about that, love."

Startled, Bridget looked down to see the old lady beaming up at her. "Did I say that out aloud?" she gasped, mortified.

"Yeah, but who could blame you?" The old lady looked dreamily over at the handsome man and sighed. "If I was fifty years younger, he'd be in trouble, that's all I can say."

Bridget giggled and chatted with the old lady until at last, she got to the top of the line and bought her food which she ate at the base of some dunes further up the beach. Every now and then she would search the water to locate the tall blond. He was easy to spot in his turquoise board shorts out in the surf catching a few waves. It was nice to watch him unobserved from her vantage point. Occasionally, she would acknowledge a twinge of guilt over looking at a man other than Jackson, and then the truth would come slamming down like a judge's gavel. Verdict - Jackson isn't yours, Bridget. He never was. He doesn't love you. It's over. Then the real Bridget would push again from within. The indignant Bridget, the proud Bridget, encouraging and boosting her confidence a smidgen further. It was a sensation she welcomed back with open arms.

From her spot on the beach, the sapphire-blue water looked so tempting, she regretted not bringing something to swim in. But there was no reason not to get at least a little bit wet. She unfolded her stiff muscles and made her way down to the water's edge, wading in till the water came up to her knees. Keeping to the shallows, Bridget splashed along, stopping here and there to pick up a pretty shell which she tucked into the pocket of her shorts. An urgent shout somewhere behind her, made Bridget turn around. Further back where she had been sitting, a woman was screaming for help. Some people were stopping and looking at her with concern. Although Bridget couldn't hear, she could see they were asking her what was the matter. Others, Bridget noticed in angry amazement, had pulled their phones out and were recording the scene. And then Bridget saw it, at the woman's feet, a small limp body lay in the sand. Without a second thought, Bridget started to run. Where were the lifeguards? She'd seen their watch tower about five hundred meters up the beach. As she ran, she shouted at anyone who would listen. "Call the lifeguards! Unconscious child on the beach!" Bridget fell momentarily and was up in an instant, sprinting as hard as her legs would carry her. Out of the corner of her eye, another figure was running up from the water. It was Turquoise board shorts, hurtling along like some kind of superhero toward the screaming woman. Bridget arrived panting heavily at the woman's side. What she saw made her heart sink.

"My boy! Help my boy! A Bluebottle stung him. I think he's allergic!"

Without answering, Bridget sank to her knees by the little boy. He looked about five and his lips were blue. Across his torso and upper arms were the tell-tale red welts of a jellyfish sting. Bluebottles were painful but not usually dangerous. If this child was experiencing anaphylactic shock, he could die. She shouted again for someone to get the lifeguards and then, summoning everything she had learned in First Aid at school, she immediately began CPR. Beside her, the boy's mother was kneeling over them now with silent tears coursing down her face. Bridget was also aware of Turquoise board shorts beside her assessing the situation.

"What's going on? Are you trained?" he was asking Bridget. She shook her head.

"Bluebottle sting. Possible allergic reaction."

"Then let me help; you breathe; I'll do the compressions."

Together, the two of them continued to work on the little boy with the hushed, expectant crowd watching on. Bridget wondered if they were making any difference at all when finally, after what seemed an age, the crowd parted for two lifeguards, who quickly assessed the situation, and took over. Relieved, Bridget and Turquoise board shorts, moved away, shaking and exhausted from the adrenaline coursing through their veins. They stood leaning on each other watching on as the lifeguards worked. Bridget found herself praying repeatedly; please God, don't let him die? The silence around them was heavy, broken only by the sounds of the lifeguards working on the little boy and the mournful call of gulls. The waves rolled into shore rhythmically as though they were trying to drum life back into the child.

A sudden noise split the quiet. A wet splutter and a weak cough, and then thank heaven, a louder choke and cough, and then a cry! An unearthly wail burst from the little boy's mother as she realized her son wasn't dead and a cheer rose from the crowd. Bridget found herself turning to congratulate Turquoise board shorts only to find that he had left. When did that happen? She scanned the beach without success. He was nowhere to be seen. Bridget turned back to watch the little boy being carried off on a stretcher. His mother paused a moment to hug her and thank her.

"Thank you so much, I think you saved my little boy's life! Please thank your boyfriend for me okay?" She hurried off to follow her son and the crowd dispersed. Bridget stood there, suddenly deflated after the intensity of the experience. For some reason, the beach had lost its attraction and her thoughts turned to the Agricultural show. Maybe it wouldn't be such a bad idea to go for an hour or two?

Half an hour later she was entering the town of Bluegum having first gone back to the motel for a change of clothes. It was easy to find the showgrounds. Street signs directing the traffic to the show were on every corner. Pedestrians seemed to have only one destination, and when she pulled into carpark she could see that there was still a bit of a queue to buy tickets. Bridget entered the grounds through an old-fashioned turnstile joining the throng of hot and tired patrons trying to navigate the crowds. The festival was in full swing with Ferris wheels and Dodgem cars, side shows, and fairy floss stands. She passed huge barns and stables which housed all of the prize winning livestock. The smell of manure wafted out making Bridget's nostrils twitch. Ugh, she thought, immediately regretting her decision. What she needed was somewhere she could just sit and be entertained for a while. Reflecting on childhood visits to the Royal Melbourne Show, a particularly fond memory popped into her head. The Grand Arena, of course! She would go and watch the parades of animals, the horse tricks, the clowns and daredevil acts and maybe even wait till evening for the firework display.

Bridget decided to just follow the general flow of pedestrians, stopping here and there to look at displays on the way. On the corner of an intersection was an old fashioned American style diner where they sold snacks and takeaway food. As she passed she could see into the diner. People were sitting, chatting and eating in the leather upholstered booths. She was hungry, but she wasn't in the mood for hotdogs. She was just about to cross the road and stop at a place selling kebabs when out of the corner of her eye she glimpsed a flash of blond hair. Bridget stopped dead in her tracks causing a man and woman to crash into her from behind.

"Watch where you're bloody going!"

Bridget wasn't sure if she apologized or not. She actually didn't care, because there, shoving a hot dog into his beautiful mouth, was Turquoise board shorts, in the American Diner! Before embarrassment, fear, or good judgment could stop her, she had climbed the few steps and walked through the glass doors. He didn't look up; he was too engrossed in his meal to notice. Bridget found herself standing by his booth with a shy grin on her face.

"Hi."

Turquoise board shorts started. His wide blue eyes opening even wider at the sight of her. "Hey!" He struggled to stand up but got hooked up on the corner of the table, jabbing his hip and making him wince. He smiled through the pain, extending his hand to her. "Hey, it's you, the CPR girl!"

"Yep, it's me. I was just passing and happened to see you. You left so quickly at the beach, I was hoping to introduce myself and thank you for your help... do you mind if I join you?"

"No, not at all, no worries, I'd enjoy you... I mean, that would be nice."

Bridget slid into the booth across from him and they appraised each other for a couple of seconds.

"I'm Bridget, and you are?"

"Daniel, Daniel Inglis."

"You say that like you're James Bond or something." Bridget ran her hand through her hair and twiddled with a loose curl at the end. "Actually, you did look a bit like James Bond running up the beach like that to save the day."

Daniel grimaced. "Oh, no, did I? How embarrassing. Well, you were doing a bit of a Wonder woman yourself. It was quite impressive."

Bridget laughed. "We should have our own show!" They were interrupted by a waitress who took Bridget's order. Bridget continued, "So, do you live locally?"

"No." Just on a trip for work and passing through. You?"

Bridget sighed, wondering how much she should say. "No, I'm not local. I guess you could say I'm a city girl looking to make a sea change. I'm on the hunt for a new place to establish some roots and start a new life." She stopped wondering if she had said too much. Daniel seemed to understand and didn't pry any further.

"That sounds quite an appealing idea actually. I think we all could benefit from starting afresh once in a while. What do you do for a crust?"

"I'm a teacher, and I run an online business writing résumés and cover letters." She narrowed her eyes at him, thinking. "Hmm, let me see if I can guess what you are. You look like you could be a doctor... am I close?"

"Well, I am in the business of taking care of people so you're right there. I guess you could say I'm a social worker of sorts."

Bridget absorbed the information in happy disbelief; this guy was almost too good to be true. A social worker meant he was someone who cared about people, not only that, he was polite, unpretentious, and of course drop dead gorgeous. And the best thing about him, she decided, was that he was the absolute opposite of Jackson. All of the feelings of longing and hurt about Jackson dissolved right there in that diner booth. It fizzled into nothing so quickly she was shocked into stark realization of what she had been succumbing herself to for the past ten months. The understanding that not only had Jackson never loved her but that she had never loved him was as plain as the nose on her face. Across from her Daniel was looking at her with one eyebrow raised and a crooked smile.

"By the look on your face, my job description doesn't meet with your approval."

"What? Oh, no! I think it's a wonderful, honorable kind of work… No, if I looked odd, I was thinking of how different you are to someone I know."

Daniel was quiet, focusing his attention on removing the cherry from the top of his Ice-cream Sundae. It slipped off the edge of his spoon and slid down the side of his glass onto the plate; his eyes traveled from his plate to the bruises on her wrists. "Is that someone you're running away from?" His blue eyes looked up and held her in a questioning gaze for a moment before licking the ice-cream off his spoon. Bridget pulled her hands back under the table, her voice was mildly indignant.

"You could say that. But not running. Yesterday I was dragging myself away, but today I can say it's over. I've left and I'm never going back."

"Good."

Bridget looked up at him. He was looking at her steadily, knowingly. She took a deep breath. "And now I'm all alone like Nellie No Friends at the Bluegum Agricultural Show. I don't suppose I could twist your arm to spend the day with me? I'd feel silly going on the roller coaster by myself."

Daniel hesitated, but only for an instant. "Consider it twisted," he said with a grin.

They spent the rest of the afternoon having more fun than Bridget had experienced in what seemed like years. Daniel was funny and intelligent and insightful with an air of confidence that was deeply appealing. Never once did he utter a sexist remark or blurt obscenities or look her over like a piece of steak, like Jackson would have. In contrast, he was the consummate gentleman, helping her onto rides, walking ahead of her in the crowds to shield her from being jostled, and opening doors for her. Once or twice when standing in a queue she would feel his hand brush against hers or his hand on her arm protectively.

After the sun went down, they took their dinner to the Grand Arena to watch the fireworks. As they stood staring mesmerized like little children at the display, Bridget felt Daniel's arms slip around her waist from behind. She leaned into him, enjoying the hard warmth of his chest against her back and his mouth near her ear. Like this, it was difficult to concentrate on the fireworks because there were fireworks of another sort going off inside her. But, fighting to the surface of her consciousness, a small voice came unsolicited from the deepest recesses of her mind. It was a voice of – what was it a voice of, caution perhaps, or was it good judgment? Don't rush it was telling her, but the voice quickly became garbled and indistinct as she pushed it back where it came from.

Their conversation became slower and quieter after that. A different kind of language had taken over. Words were replaced by holding hands and shy caresses. As they walked back to Daniel's car the air was electric with the question – what next? There was a choice to be made. Was Daniel making the same choice? What was he thinking? She looked at him sideways out of the corner of her eye, as he fumbled with the car keys. He's nervous too, she realized. The trip home in the car was silent except for snippets of polite small talk. Neither of them wanted to destroy the mood, they were heading toward one conclusion for the night and they both knew it.

Daniel walked Bridget to her door; the light above had blown and they were standing, conveniently, in the shadows, away from prying eyes. She wondered if there was any point going through the usual end of date etiquette of thanking Daniel for a nice time, the invitation for a nightcap etc. He was still behind her, so she turned to face him and lifted her face to his. What she saw on his face startled her somewhat. His eyes that had been bright and blue all day, were now almost black; his pupils dilated to their fullest. There was an intensity there that both frightened her and bound her, unable to look away. She ran her tongue over her lips in anticipation and his eyes dropped to her mouth. When he spoke, his voice was hoarse.

"You have the most beautiful mouth."

Bridget's lips curled into a softly parted smile and she leaned in closer. He was going to kiss her. She closed her eyes and waited, focusing all of her attention on her mouth in anticipation. The night breeze on her moist lips was cool, and then his lips were there, warm, firm and full on hers. His arms went around her and lifted her up so that her toes were barely touching the ground. He held her so effortlessly that she let herself relax into the kiss. This was more like it; so much nicer than Jackson's hurried, rough embraces. A new idea came to her mind, wouldn't it be nice to leave it here and to let it remain sweet and romantic, to softly say goodnight and close the door in anticipation of another date? But as Daniel's kisses became more urgent, her resolve began to weaken. Self-control had never been her forte. She broke the kiss and pulled away. "Stay with me?" she whispered. Daniel nodded and followed her into the dark motel room and closed the door behind him with a click.

She was in a strange house with a corridor flanked by walls with garish lime wallpaper. The color made her nauseous. Along the walls were dozens of doors leading to dark rooms, which she entered panicked and fevered, looking for something, but she didn't know what. "I'm running out of time, running out of time!" The words ran in a loop over and over in her head, but the further she ran down the corridor the smaller it got and every room became more cramped, stifling her and filling her with desperate dread, until finally she was wedged tight and suffocating at the pointed end of the corridor, curled up in a ball.

Bridget woke with a start sitting bolt upright in the dawn light, covered in perspiration and her chest heaving. The dream, which was a reoccurring one, was still fresh in her mind, but she knew if she waited a minute it would fade. Then she remembered Daniel. Jerking her head around, she stared at the other side of the bed. It was rumpled, but empty. She scanned the room. He was gone. He had left nothing behind. A small white object on the sheet beside her caught her eye. It was the butt of a ticket for the roller coaster ride from the day before. Bridget lay back on the pillow staring with unseeing eyes at the tiny shred of paper. Last night had not been what she had expected. She had expected to wake up full and replete with Prince Charming breathing softly beside her. Instead, the experience had been furtive and intense. Daniel's set jaw and black eyes swam before her. There had been nothing magical about last night as she had hoped. A ball of regret began to form in the pit of her stomach. It was too soon after Jackson. She had known that last night. Why couldn't she just say no to men? Nick was going to have something to say about this when she told him.

The thought of unburdening herself to Nick gave her some comfort. The red digits on the bedside clock glowed 6:23; a bit early but he'd be getting up to get ready for work soon anyway. His phone rang out. She was hesitating, wondering whether she should try again when her phone began to vibrate; Nick's photo coming up on her screen. She swiped the screen with relief.

"Hi, it's me." Nick's voice was heavy with sleep.

"Hi, me, sorry for waking you up. I just needed to talk to my best mate."

"Hmm. Are you okay?"

Bridget could hear him yawning and stretching on the other end of the line.

"Yeah, I'm safe but just depressed and sick of myself. I'm so stupid, Nick."

"What happened?"

"I met this guy."

Nick moaned in exasperation. "What? A guy? Bridget, it has been three days since you left Jackson. Three days! You have no business getting involved with any guy for any reason right now. And then, realizing that he hadn't heard her out, his tone softened. "I'm sorry, I didn't give you a chance to explain, go ahead."

"No, you are right to be exasperated. I met a guy, a really nice guy, but I rushed things and he ended up staying the night. He didn't hurt me, it's not like he's a serial killer or anything, I just feel stupid for being so desperate and having no self-control." Her voice began to quiver with emotion. "I've forgotten what's good about me, Nick. I'm just sick of myself."

Nick didn't answer right away and when he did his voice was tender. "There's plenty that's good about you Bridget." But you have to learn how to be alone and happy before you can be with someone and be happy. There are good men out there, but you have to be willing to change your expectations. My mom always said that the best apples were at the top of the tree and the hardest ones to find and she was right." The silence on Bridget's end told Daniel she was crying. "You're the best friend I've ever had Bridget and I hate to see you sad. I think you're crazy sometimes, but I'll always be here for you. What are you going to do now? Will you come home?"

A part of Bridget wanted to go home, but she had left for a reason, to learn about herself and to reinvent herself where nobody had any preconceived notions about her. "No Nick. I'm going to find somewhere to settle up here and make a go of it. Thanks for listening to me, you're my bestie and I love you." Nick's voice was soft in reply. "I love you too."

Once Bridget was dressed, she went into Bluegum and bought some supplies, including a map of Queensland. Her motel room had been cleaned and the bed made when she returned. It matched her mood. She felt energized. It was finally time to leave her old life and her old mistakes behind her. But she needed a place to lay down roots. She spread the map out over the small circular dining table, holding it in place with the pepper and salt shakers on two corners and the sugar bowl on another. She rummaged in her shopping bag and ripped open a crackling plastic package containing a brand new red felt pen. She leaned close to locate Bluegum on the map and placed a small red dot there, then, raising the pen like a dagger, she shut her eyes and dropped her arm, randomly onto the map. It had landed about two inches away from the Bluegum dot. "Good, not too far to drive then," she muttered. She squinted and shifted her head to the side to see the name of her new hometown. Currawong about an hour away from Bluegum. She liked the name of the town immediately. Currawong, one of her favourite Australian birds, like a large black crow with patches of white on the tips of its wings was a good omen to her. She had no idea what was at Currawong, maybe she would arrive to find nothing, but she was going to go anyway and see what happened.

The trip was uneventful, but as she drew closer to her destination, she was pleased to see green fields, rather than the harsh yellow bushlands she had been expecting. A large sign on the side of the road said: "You are entering Currawong – pop 5000." She instantly felt like she had gone back 60 years. The houses were vintage weatherboard houses, circa 1950 with immaculate gardens and pristine driveways. Many of the homes were on acreage with a couple of horses grazing back from the road. The main strip was fairly modern but it only took a few minutes to drive through the center of town and then she was back out in the country.

Being careful to keep to the speed limit, she headed for the motel she had booked into back in Opal Bay. "Turn left in 100 meters," said the ever polite voice on her GPS. As Bridget turned left she admired a sweet old bluestone church on the corner. A group of parishioners were in the front weeding and tending the garden. They were an assorted group of moms, dads, children, teenagers and old age pensioners, all working together in a steady rhythm. With her windows rolled down, she could hear laughter and chatter coming from the group. Something inside her wished she could park the car and join in; there seemed to be such a spirit of belonging amongst them.

That night as she lay in her motel bed, looking through the newspaper for rental properties, she reflected on the little church again. As a little girl, her parents had taken her every week to church and she had enjoyed their time together as a family. She remembered the solemn feelings she held in her heart, even as a child, for the church and everything it stood for. She missed the reverent prayers, the quiet atmosphere, and the hope it all inspired. Maybe that was what was missing in her life? How far had she drifted away from her core beliefs? How much had she let the whims and wishes of others influence her away from what she held to be true? She made the decision there and then, that she would attend church services the next Sunday. Bridget felt much lighter over the next couple of days. She felt good about looking inside herself and facing her demons head on. It was nice to let the misery go and to commit to change. It felt like her soul was being washed clean in her resolve to be happy.

On Sunday morning, she dressed for church. Her packing had been abysmal with absolutely nothing that could pass as suitable for church, so the day before, she had bought herself a new dress befitting her mood. It was a crisp cotton dress with a fitted bodice and wide knee-length skirt in pale yellow. She matched it with a pair of summery slingback white stilettos and finished the look by pulling her auburn hair up into a long ponytail, making her look every bit as wholesome as she hoped she would. Looking herself over in the mirror she raised an eyebrow at her reflection. "This is it, Bridget. Don't let me down."

The walk to church seemed to be straight out of a Disney movie. The sun was shining, the birds singing, the breeze cool and refreshing. Families were walking to church together in their Sunday best. Bridget held back a little. She wanted to be the last to walk into the chapel so that she wouldn't be an object of curiosity to the others. At first, when she entered the chapel she was blinded in the cool dark after the brilliance of the outside sunshine. The chapel was nearly full friends and families in soft conversation, waiting for the reverend to emerge from the vestry. Bridget quietly took a seat in the last pew. Thankfully nobody had noticed her yet. She sat in quiet meditation, while the organist treated them to soft prelude music. It was rare that Bridget felt confident about one of her decisions, but today, she was convinced she was in the right place.

The prelude music faded and the congregation turned their faces in unison toward the vestry door. A soft click of a door latch at the side of the chapel released a beam of yellow light from within and emerging from the light, a tall figure, so tall and broad he had to bend his head to avoid hitting the top of the door. It was a blond head. From where she sat, Bridget couldn't see his face, only the back of his blond head and his black robes. Bridget's heart began to beat quicker. There was an uncomfortable sensation bubbling up from her stomach to her throat. The reverend was looking far too familiar for her liking. Then as the organist began to play the opening hymn, he turned around to face the congregation. Bridget took an audible gasp of air. Daniel! It was Daniel!

The congregation rose from their seats in a synchronized swoosh. Somewhere on the right side of the chapel, someone dropped their hymnbook with a loud clatter, but Bridget barely heard it; the chorus of voices around her was a muffled behind the blood whooshing through her ears. She felt faint and leaned forward to rest her head on the back of the pew in front of her. Daniel, a priest? Shame and anger threatened to drown her as she remembered with embarrassment their night together. If she'd known, she would have never.... How dare he not tell her? The shame began to dissipate. He was the one breaking his vows. She wasn't party to that. She looked up at him standing at the pulpit. Was he going to stand up there and preach from the Bible now?

The hymn ended and the congregation sat, waving fans in the heat, all eyes watching Daniel in rapt expectation. Bridget was glad that the chapel was full. It was unlikely that Daniel would see her sitting down in the back row, but leaving was out of the question; firstly, he would see her leave and think her a coward and secondly, she wanted to confront him. He started to speak and Bridget, in spite of herself was impressed. He wasn't preachy at all. He spoke of kindness and acceptance, service and dedication. He told amusing anecdotes that made the congregation chuckle, he mentioned people by name, he spoke of his own weaknesses. Bridget was starting to soften. Maybe the night with her was a one-off? Maybe, like everyone else, he had weaknesses that he was trying to work through? As the hour passed, so did her indignation. She gazed at Daniel. He was beautiful she had to admit. Maybe there could be a future with him? If she were to approach him and if he were willing, they could start afresh, and she would never ask him to overstep the boundaries of his faith. Nick's words nagged at her conscience, "you have to learn to be alone." "Oh, shut up, Nick," she mumbled out loud, making the people in front of her turn and stare.

After the service, Bridget, made her way against the stream of people leaving the chapel, up towards the pulpit, where Daniel was tidying up and preparing to leave. She arrived at the front just as he was heading towards the vestry.

"Reverend Inglis?"

Daniel turned swiftly with a ready smile, which fell comically as soon as he recognized her. "Yes? Oh!"

"Surprised to see me?"

Daniel's face froze into a stiff smile, but his eyes were boring into hers heavy with meaning. He spoke in urgent tones through his stiff smile like a ventriloquist. "Can't talk now." He glanced over Bridget's shoulder at someone approaching from behind. And then she heard the sound that made her blood run cold; a little girl's voice over the din of the departing congregation.

"Daddy!"

Like an ax dropping onto the executioner's block, Bridget's expression dropped into one of quiet fury. Not this. There would be no forgiving for this! She looked over her shoulder to see a little girl of about four, with honey colored curls running toward Daniel. He stood stiffly as his daughter hugged his legs. Following the little girl was a dark haired woman with a babe in arms. The woman approached her with a friendly smile. "Hello, you must be new? I'm Carrie Inglis, welcome!" She offered her hand to Bridget who did her best to hitch a believable looking smile onto her face. Whatever had happened was not this woman's fault, and she was not going to do anything that could possibly hurt her any further. "Hi, Carrie, nice to meet you."

Carrie's face was open, gazing directly into Bridget's eyes. "It's always good to have new people join us," she turned to Daniel, "isn't it honey?" But Daniel was already half way out of the chapel with his little girl in tow. Carrie laughed. "What's his rush? He's usually hanging around talking for ages after church. So, tell me about yourself, where are you staying?" She was so genuine that Bridget found herself wavering between shock and anger at Daniel and an irresistible connection with his wife. Overriding these two emotions was an overwhelming desire to get away, to be alone where she could lick her wounds and somehow come to terms with what had happened. She jotted down her address and phone number for Carrie and then making her excuses she made her way back to the motel room. It wasn't until she was alone that the full impact of what Daniel had subjected her to hit her. All of the excuses she had tried to make for him, fell flat and lifeless. He was a liar and a cheater and cheating on one of the loveliest ladies she had ever met and only a few weeks after she'd given birth to a new baby!

Like the voice of her conscience sitting on her shoulder, Nick's voice came to her mind. "It takes two to tango," he was saying, "Daniel didn't do this on his own."

"But I didn't know he was married!" she cried out to the room at large. "Did you know anything about him before you invited him home?" came Nick's steady voice again.

Bridget looked at her phone. If she had Nick's voice berating her in her head, she may as well call him and get the confession over and done with. He was going to find out about this at some point anyway, and she really needed his advice. When he answered his voice was cautious but hopeful.

"Hey Bridget, is this call to just say hi to your best friend because you miss me, or have you got bad news?"

Bridget sighed. "Bad news. He is a priest. A married priest with two children."

"Who, what? No, not the guy from the other night? How do you know?"

"I randomly attended his church today. How's that for serendipity?"

There was silence on the line for a moment. "Maybe serendipity, or maybe a life lesson? Maybe a chance to make things right? Wow, Bridge' what a shock. What's his wife like? Did she find out?"

"She's an absolute darling. Anybody who could willingly hurt a person like her has got to have something wrong with them, and no, thankfully, she doesn't know anything."

"What are you going to do?"

Bridget asked herself the same question. What was she going to do? She felt she had been directed to this little town, and directed to the church. Should she let Daniel's presence influence her own journey? No, why should he have a say? Maybe Currawong had happier surprises up its sleeve for her. The decision formed and settled in her heart. "I'm going to stay," she answered.

The week that followed was a blur. Carrie contacted her on the Tuesday with a fabulous rental opportunity. An elderly aunt and uncle were going overseas for six months and needed a house-sitter. The situation was perfect, she wouldn't have to buy furniture, the rent was cheap and the house boasted a backyard shady with glorious, mauve, Jacarandas and a wrap-around veranda, perfect for entertaining or working on her laptop. By Thursday she had moved in and made friends with neighbors and been invited for tea. By 10 o'clock that evening she was brushing her teeth getting ready for bed and feeling appreciative and hopeful for the future.

She had just pulled on an old t-shirt and a pair of Jackson's old boxers when she heard what she thought was a quiet knock on the front door. She stopped and cocked an ear to listen. Who would be knocking this late? The neighbor's dog started to bark. Bridget mentally retraced her going-to-bed ritual, had she locked all the doors? Confident that she had, she sank down onto her bed.

There it was again. Someone was definitely knocking. Padding silent as a cat in her bare feet, she approached the front door. She let out a sigh, grateful that she had taken the time to slip the safety chain into place. Another quiet knock, this time, more urgent than the last. Bridget pressed her face against the spy hole and switched on the porch light. Daniel's face, nervous and handsome was there, staring straight at the keyhole.

Jerking her face back, Bridget took a moment to decide what to do. What on earth could he want? She imagined he probably wanted to come to beg her to stay quiet about their night together. What a creep! In one swift movement, she had yanked the door open, the safety chain stopping it from opening further than four inches.

"What are you doing here?" She peered at him through the gap with narrowed eyes.

Daniel's smile was sheepish. "Bridget, I was hoping we could talk?"

"What about?"

"Us." He tried to stare seductively through the small gap in the doorway. He looked like an idiot. "I can't forget our night together, can you?" When she said nothing, he continued. "Can I come in? I'm feeling a bit exposed here under the porch light."

Bridget couldn't believe the brazen cheek of the man. "I've got nothing to hide, Daniel, and there isn't any 'us' as you put it." Her words were as sharp as razor blades. "And you've got a bloody cheek coming here and expecting me to be complicit in hurting a beautiful person like Carrie! I'm not in the business of dating married men and even if you don't appreciate your beautiful family, I do. Now rack off, before I call Carrie and tell her everything!" She slammed the door, breathing deeply with anger. Perhaps she should tell Carrie. She didn't deserve to be treated with this kind of callous, disrespect. She deserved to be rid of Daniel. Bridget imagined with satisfaction, Carrie confronting Daniel and kicking him out on the street. But there in the background of her fantasy was a small four-year-old girl crying and a baby who would only ever know weekend visits from his father.

The picture was so sad; she knew that she would never tell. She refused to add to her list of regrets, the destruction of a family.

She didn't hear from Daniel again. In spite of the drama, Bridget felt that Currawong was going to be good for her. It filled her with pride to face her fears, to confront her weaknesses and direct her attention to the needs of others for a while. Carrie was showing her that. Every day, in one way or another, Carrie was doing something to help. It didn't matter if it was a human need or a stray animal, everyone who needed it, got a dose of her kindness and attention. It inspired Bridget to do the same.

The wet season hit Queensland earlier than usual and out of the blue. One afternoon, a couple of weeks after moving in, Bridget sat in her study, staring at the torrential downpour outside. The power was out, there was no TV, and the battery on her laptop was flat and it looked like she would be forced to indulge in a lazy afternoon curled up on the couch with a book. Her phone rang. On the other end, she could hear Carrie over the din of the rain. It sounded like she was inside a tin shed. Carrie was shouting, but Bridget could only catch intermittent words. "Help – deliver shopping – old – car- time?"

Bridget yelled back. "I couldn't really hear what you said, but if you need my help, come and get me. I'll be waiting at my place!" Bridget caught a muffled "Thanks!" and hung up the phone. Fifteen minutes later, she was in the front seat of

Carrie's car in a yellow raincoat. "Okay, what am I helping you with today?"

Carrie grabbed Bridget's hand and squeezed it. "You're an angel for coming. I just need to deliver these meals to some elderly shut-ins today. Their usual delivery service is canceled due to the rain and I couldn't bear it if they went without a meal or a friendly face today. With your help, I'll be able to get it done in half the..." A loud screeching of wheels forced them to turn in terror to their right. A truck had lost control and was sliding from the opposite lane directly into their path. Before the truck slammed into them, Bridget caught a glimpse of the desperate expression on the face of the other driver. And then there was nothing.

She was in the strange house with the corridors again. This time, there was pain. Bridget resisted. She didn't want to have this dream but have it she would. Stretching away into the distance the corridor elongated. The doors came into view, beckoning her to start searching for that elusive something. She tried to grip the walls but her hands slid off, slick and wet. Against her will, she found herself at the first door. I'm running out of time... out of time... Someone was calling her from far away, "Bridget!" they called. I can't find you! She was rummaging through the room, searching. "Bridget!" The voice was louder now, from somewhere nearby, "Please wake up!" She was frantic. Help me find you!

Bridget felt herself emerge from the coma as though traveling an elevator one floor at a time. When she got to the top, her eyes opened. All around her were blurred moving shapes and muffled sounds. Only one shape directly in front of her face stayed still. She focused on it and waited for the blurriness to go away. Gradually, the shape became more distinct, the lines sharper, it was a face. It was Nick's face, wet with tears and he was smiling. Suddenly his face was next to hers and he was sobbing. She didn't know why. But now that Nick was there, everything was going to be all right.

Nick was there every day over the next two weeks in the hospital. Bridget had a concussion, a few broken ribs, a collapsed lung and her spleen had been removed. Nick told her that she had been in a coma for three days after the accident. He had taken the first flight to Queensland and had been by her side ever since. Carrie hadn't fared so well. She was still in a coma in intensive care with multiple broken bones and a head injury.

On her day of discharge, Bridget made her way to Carrie's hospital room. Daniel was by her bedside. His face was white. He looked at Bridget with eyes frantic and bloodshot. She realized in an instant that he was already receiving his punishment, nothing she could say could make him feel worse than he did right now. So, he loved his wife after all; or was this just guilt? Perhaps it was not her place to judge. She took a few ginger steps into the room and gripped the bars at the foot of Carrie's bed.

"How is she?"

Daniel leaned his elbows on the bed and rested his face in his hands. "Not good."

"I think we may have both learned the same lesson from this experience, Daniel. Since I met Carrie I've been judging you for taking your wife for granted. But I now realize that I've been taking someone for granted too, someone who has loved me my whole life and has watched and waited patiently while I've repeatedly thrown myself at people who didn't hold a candle to him. Buddha once said, 'The trouble is; you think you have time,' well now we both know that everything that is important can be taken in an instant. There is no time to waste, we only have now." Bridget turned to go and then hesitating she murmured without looking back. "Take care Daniel, I'll keep you and Carrie in my prayers."

The sunshine was bright in her hospital room when she walked stiffly through the door. Nick had his back to her; he was packing her pajamas and underwear into a duffle bag. Bridget eased her sore body into the chair by the bed and watched him. His big hands were awkward as he fumbled with her silky underwear. His brow was furrowed, his honest, open eyes, tense with the effort, his upturned boyish nose wrinkled in determination. From under her ribs, a wave of peace and security flooded her, filling her up until her heart felt like it would burst. She let out a delighted laugh. Why hadn't she been able to see it before? All the years of pain and misery looking for Mr. Right when she had the perfect man right under her nose the whole time. "I love Nick." Saying it to herself made it all the truer. She loved Nick and when the time was right she would tell him.

"There, he said with finality, zipping up the duffle bag. Where would you like to go next, my lady?"

"Home, please, Nick," she answered, rising to her feet. "Take me home."

RECKLESSLY AMISH
SAMANTHA COLLIER

Chapter One
  Loss

John puffed slightly as he walked over the plain, taking off his black hat to wipe sweat from his brow. This shouldn't be happening. Still at least twenty minutes from home. His father was going to be angry.

Well, he hadn't planned for it. When the wheel had started wobbling on the buggy as he cantered along the familiar dirt road, he had slowed down. He had done everything that he could think of to get the thing home. Yes, he knew that his father had told him to adjust it days ago, but he had just plumb forgot. And then, of course, it had completely left the axle, causing the buggy to veer off into the ditch. He didn't have anything on him to fix it. So he had left it, and started walking. The horses weren't up to bare back riding.

He knew that this was a short cut; he had heard people talking about it. Veer over the plains, rather than take the road. He was still unfamiliar with the area, but he knew enough landmarks to be okay. Well, he had no other choice. He had to get home, and quickly.

It was only supposed to be a quick trip into town, to get a few things his mother needed for the Easter dinner. They had relatives arriving for the feast, all the way from Indiana, where they had recently moved from. His parents were counting on him. And then, this had to happen.

John stopped, frowning, as he surveyed the landscape. He thought he was going the right way, but it all looked the same. With a pained sigh, he started off again. Luckily, it was a perfect spring day, not a cloud in the sky. If a trifle hot.

He set off, again. It shouldn't be too much further, surely?

And that's when he saw the figure on horseback, riding over the plain like it was being pursued by half of the state. A black horse, tall and handsome. He couldn't quite make out the rider; could just see the figure crouched over the horse, spurring it on to greater speed. Really, the person was riding the horse way too fast. Yes, it was an open plain, but John knew the hard way that there were many dips and hidden holes here. He had stepped into a couple, by accident.

If the horse stepped into one, it would lose its footing entirely, and at the speed they were going, throw the rider clean off. It would also be lucky not to break its leg, and everyone knew that was the worst thing that could happen to a horse. It would be the death of the creature.

The rider approached, still at full speed. The person could see him...surely? But it didn't slow down. Instead, it approached him with such ferocity that John instinctively dived to the left.

His hat fell off, rolling down an embankment. He got up, seething with anger. The fool had almost caused another accident. He watched as the rider reined in the horse, then turned it back toward him.

"Are you alright?" The figure atop the horse gazed down at him.

John looked up, about to give the man a piece of his mind, when the words froze on his lips. It wasn't a man. No, it was a girl, and an Amish girl, at that. Still with her prayer *kapps* on her head, although it had become slightly dislodged by the wild ride. As had her hair; instead of a neat bun, it was flowing down her back.

John gaped. He had simply never seen a girl ride like that, with no awareness of her surroundings or her appearance. Who on earth was she?

"I said, are you alright?" The girl's voice sounded impatient. Well, that took the cake. She had almost ploughed into him with her horse, and there was no apology.

John brushed off his dark pants. There were scuff marks on them; his mother was not going to be happy. He was dressed in his best clothes for the feast, not his regular work ones. This day was just getting worse.

"No thanks to you," John spat, glaring up at the girl. "What do you think you were doing, riding the horse so fast towards me?"

The girl had the gall to laugh, throwing her head back so that her hair fell down her back.

"I thought you would move," she said, her eyes glittering. "Don't worry, you were never in any danger. I've been riding horses since I could walk."

"Well, then, you should know that riding one that fast on a pock holed plain is a bad idea," John answered, sourly. He waited for the apology that was his due. But she simply looked at him, smiling bemusedly.

"Who are you?" she asked, cocking her head to the side as she assessed him. "I've never seen you before."

"John Miller," he said, stiffly. "My family has only just moved here, a month ago."

"Are you living at the old Yoder farmhouse?"

"*Jah.*" He scratched his head, looking up at her. "That's where I am heading, now. The wheel came off my buggy on the road, and I was told this was a shortcut."

"A shortcut to where?" She laughed, again. "You are heading in the wrong direction. You need to go that way." She pointed west. He looked, confused. He was sure he had been going the right way.

"Well, John Miller," she laughed, grabbing the reins, "good luck!" She took off at high speed, flying back over the plain in the opposite direction.

He watched her, his jaw open, riding like the wind until she was a mere speck on the horizon.

John picked up his hat, dusty on the ground. Who on earth was she? He had never known an Amish girl to be quite so.... reckless. He was used to demure and apologetic girls, who would never ride alone, and certainly not in the way that she had. Maybe the Amish girls were different in this part of the country? He hadn't really spoken to any, not yet. His family had attended a few church services, but he hadn't really socialised. He thought of Miriam, the girl he had been sweet on back in Indiana. Miriam would never have dreamt of riding like that, and would certainly have never spoken the way that the girl had.

He eventually got to the farmhouse, his mood sour. The family were all assembled at the table, waiting for him. His father stood up, frowning, watching his son walk through the door.

"Where have you been, John?" The older man's jaw tightened.

"It is a long story," John sighed. "The wheel came off the buggy, and I had to walk over the plain. Then I almost got knocked over by a horse. A girl on a black horse, riding like the wind." He shook his head, not believing his own words.

His mother had got to her feet. "You look a mess," she said. "Go and clean up." She sat back down. "Did you say a girl on a black horse? I have heard of her. The church elders of the district have talked of her, and not in a good way."

"What is her name?" John asked. He could still picture her in his mind's eye, hair flowing, eyes glittering.

"Sarah Glick?" His mother frowned, trying to remember. "*Jah*, I am sure that is her name. She is a wild one, that is for sure. You were lucky to walk away from her unscathed by the sound of it, John."

Sarah. The wild girl, who rode like a man. Well, he would make sure that he had nothing to do with her, ever again. A girl needed to be demure, and she didn't seem to know the meaning of the word.

As John walked off to the bathroom to wash, he tried to dislodge the vision of her from his mind. But she stayed with him, all through the lunch, and the tedious rest of the day, going back to fix the buggy, his father haranguing him the whole way.

***

Sarah dismounted Racer, giving the sweating black horse a kiss on his nose. "Thank you," she whispered. "That was a wonderful ride."

She waked into the house, tossing off her *kapps* as she went. Where was Mamm?

Right at that moment, her mother walked out of the kitchen, wiping flour on her apron. She stopped short when she saw her daughter, frowning.

"Sarah," she said, through gritted teeth, "where is your *kapps*? And your hair! It has come completely undone."

Sarah laughed. "It is always does," she said, nonchalantly. "The silly *kapps* can't contain it."

"Have you been riding too fast again?" Her mother had her hands on her hips as she looked at her.

Sarah's eyes flashed. "Why do you have to keep harping on about it?" she said, her voice raised. "I like to ride fast! And so does Racer."

"Sarah, it isn't seemly..."

Sarah rounded on her mother. "Why?" she shouted. "I have been hearing this forever! Who says that just because I am a girl I can't ride fast?"

Her mother sighed, closing her eyes. "We have talked about it many times," she said. "A girl in our community has to be meek, or at least not as wild as you are. You want to stay in our community, don't you?"

"*Jah*," admitted Sarah, breathing heavily. "You know that I do! I just can't understand why I can't be myself. Why are there all these silly rules and regulations? Why can a boy do what he likes but a girl can't?"

Her mother sighed, again. "It is just the way it is," she whispered. "It has always been that way. If you choose to be in our community, you must be respectful. People already gossip about you too much. It hurts your father, and myself."

Sarah rolled her eyes. "Small minded people," she spat. "Why do you care what they say?" She turned away, walking to the stairs. "I have to change."

Her mother watched her walk away, in despair. "Sarah," she called. "Rebecca needs you to mind the children, tomorrow."

Sarah's hand tightened on the balustrade. Not again. She really didn't enjoy looking after her sister's children. Oh, it might get better when they were older, and she could talk to them, and they could answer back. Have a conversation. She loved her niece and nephew, but babies bored her. So much mess and crying. Sarah preferred older children, who could come riding and skating with her.

"Do I have to?" she sighed, looking back at her mother.

"*Jah*," her mother answered. "You really do. I must finish my quilts for the sale, and Katie is busy, as well. It won't be for long, but you will have to get there early."

"Alright." Sarah continued up the stairs, not looking back again. Her mother watched her for a moment, then sighed heavily and went back into the kitchen.

Sarah collapsed across her bed. Another tedious day of child minding, when all she wanted to do was ride. It was such lovely weather; there was nothing she loved more in the world, than racing across the plains on Racer. He enjoyed it, too. Tomorrow was supposed to be wonderful, and now she would be cooped up inside her sister's house, trying to entertain a nine-month-old and a toddler.

Suddenly, the vision of the man on the plain today flashed through her mind. John Miller. He had looked at her like she was something from another world. Disapproving, as everyone was; Sarah had seen the sour look on his face. It was disappointing. She had thought that because he was new to the district, he might have an open mind. But all he saw was a girl on a horse, riding too fast, with a crooked prayer *kapps* and dislodged hair.

A pity. He was very handsome. Tall, with dark hair. Intriguing. Sarah mulled the vision of him over in her mind.

***

"Sarah, make sure you get into those corners," her mother said, depositing the bucket and mop at her feet. Then she walked out of the kitchen.

Sarah sighed dramatically, staring at the bucket. Tedious chores, before the day had even begun. Not that there was much to look forward to, anyway. Just babysitting.

She put the mop into the bucket, then slopped water on the floor, spreading it around disinterestedly. She didn't care what her mother said; there was no way she was moving stuff around. A quick going over with it, and then she was out of here.

Sarah hated housework, even more than babysitting, and that was saying something. Why couldn't she just be free to ride all day, the wind in her face, feeling the ground thunder beneath Racer's hooves?

At last. Mopping done, Sarah rushed out of the house, heading toward the stables. He would be getting restless. He always enjoyed a morning talk, even if she wasn't able to ride out. Racer. He had been her horse since she was twelve years old, and she liked him better than anyone.

She saddled him up, talking to him as she did so. "Not a long ride today, Racer," she said. "More's the pity. We have to head to Rebecca's to look after the babies." Racer looked at her with his deep brown eyes, seeming to sense the sorrow in her. He nudged her gently.

She was just about to head out, when her mother stopped her. "I don't want to hear any reports from people about you," she said, looking up at Sarah in the saddle. "No wild rides. Straight to your sister's house, young lady."

Sarah rolled her eyes. "Of course," she said. She picked up the reins, spurring Racer out of the stable.

It was a beautiful day, just as she had known it would be. Wildflowers bloomed everywhere; the trees swayed in the distance. Sarah stopped, breathing in the scent. She just felt more alive, somehow, out in nature. It was unnatural to be cooped up inside, tending babies and doing eternal housework. How did most women deal with it, after they were married?

She would never marry, she decided suddenly. At least, then, she wouldn't have to be a slave to a man and the children that would inevitably come. But the alternative didn't really appeal to her, either: being a spinster maid, living with her parents forever, at her mother's beck and call. What to do?

She wouldn't think about it, at all. She would just enjoy the ride. She spurred Racer on, heading across the plains towards her sister's farmhouse.

The wind felt so good. Surely one little ride, where she let Racer stretch his legs, couldn't hurt? She would still be able to get to Rebecca's on time.

Decision made, she spurred him on, flying across the plain. Freedom. A wide smile spread across her face, lodging there. There was no better feeling in the world.

The world whizzed past her, blurring. Racer picked up speed.

Suddenly, he stopped, rearing up. What was it? She barely had time to see the snake, as she flew over the horse's head, landing with a thud on the ground.

She sat up, slowly. The world was spinning. Had she knocked her head? She tried to get up, but it was all too much. She had to sit back down again.

"Are you alright?"

She jumped, almost leaping out of her skin. A figure in black loomed over her. She squinted, trying to make out who it was. Where on earth had they materialised from? She hadn't seen anyone on the plain, not even in the distance.

Then, she knew. She remembered. It was the man she had seen yesterday, John Miller.

"*Jah*, I think so," she said ruefully, rubbing her head. "I don't know what happened."

"A snake is what happened," John said. "I saw it as I was running over to you."

"A snake?" Sarah wrinkled up her nose. "But it's too early for them."

"It's because of the warm weather we've been having," he said. "They come out earlier." He crouched down, looking at her. "You were very lucky. I saw you go clear over your horse's head. Have you any injuries?"

Sarah tried to concentrate on his voice. But the sight of him, crouching down close to her, made her catch her breath. She had been right. He was a very handsome man, and she was enjoying the look of concern that was in his face as he stared at her.

"I think so," she said, gingerly. Maybe he would carry her in his arms? The thought made her glow, for a moment. Then she shook her head at her own muddled thinking.

"Try to stand up," he said. She did so, feeling woozy. But at least she was on her feet, which was something.

"Where were you going?" John asked now, reaching out to steady her. The touch of his hand on hers made her heart thump. What on earth was happening to her? It must be because of the fall. It had addled her wits, temporarily.

"To my sister's," she answered. It seemed so long ago that she had set out for Rebecca's. Was she late? That was all she needed. Rebecca would complain to their mother, and she would never hear the end of it.

"Do you want me to help you get there?" he asked, frowning. "Or do you want to go home?"

Sarah grimaced. If she headed home, her mother would scold her all day about her recklessness. No, better to push on to Rebecca's. At least, then, she could salvage the situation. A little.

"I need to get there," she said, starting to walk. She turned back to look at him. "Why are you out here?"

He blushed, slightly. Why, she didn't know. "I was just going for a walk," he said, slowly. Why wouldn't he meet her eyes? It was like he wasn't telling her the truth. But why would that be? She shook her head, slightly. She was being fanciful, again.

She went up to Racer, grabbing his reins, talking to him soothingly. Then she put her foot in the stirrup.

"What are you doing?" John approached her quickly. "You can't ride. You've had a nasty fall. I will walk with you. We can lead the horse."

Sarah turned to him, astonished. "But I will be late," she said, gritting her teeth. "And I am perfectly fine!"

"Why are you so stubborn?" he said, frowning at her. "Your sister will understand why you are late when we explain it to her."

Sarah shook her head. She was appalled to find tears had sprung into her eyes. "You don't understand," she said, bitterly. "She will know why I fell, and so why I am late, and then she will start scolding me, as everyone does!" A single tear fell down on her cheek. Oh, this was so frustrating! She wasn't one of those girls who cried at the drop of a hat. She rarely cried over anything. Why then, did she feel as if she were about start sobbing like silly Grace Fisher, the cry baby back at school?

John leant over, stroking her arm. She looked up at him, appalled to see sympathy in his eyes. Yes, he was feeling sorry for her. He must think she was like all the other girls he had ever met.

"Sarah, it's alright," he said, soothingly.

"How do you know my name?" she said, sniffling. "I never told you yesterday."

John started. "I told my family about you, when I eventually got home," he said, carefully.

Sarah's eyes widened. "Oh, I see," she said, in a disappointed voice. "Of course. Everyone has heard of me, even people who are new to the district. Silly Sarah Glick, who rides her horse too fast, dislikes babies and hates housework."

John smiled. "Well, I didn't know you hated housework," he said. He stared at her, his eyes glowing. Sarah felt her breath stop, again.

"Why does everyone disapprove of me?" she burst out, gazing at John. As if she expected an answer! He would just start lecturing her, the same as everyone else. He had done so, yesterday. She was so used to it she barely noticed it anymore.

"I suppose," he said, slowly, "because you are different to the other girls in our faith. People want everyone to be the same, and feel the same."

Sarah gasped. "*Jah*," she breathed. "That is so true!" She felt sorry for herself. She was a duckling in a swan's nest, there was no doubt about it. Did this John understand that? He seemed to.

"I think you are wonderful," he blurted, gazing at her. "But you should be careful with your riding. I would hate to see you get hurt."

"You think I am wonderful?" Sarah breathed. She gazed at him. Maybe he wasn't like all the others.

But then, he had told her to be careful, as well. And was that a slight frown on his face?

"You can escort me to my sisters," she said, stiffly. "Thank you for coming to my service. I appreciate it."

She started walking off, leading Racer.

She didn't see the look of longing that John Miller gave her, as he slowly followed her.

***

Her sister was down the steps of her veranda as soon as they arrived.

"Sarah! Where on earth have you been? You are over an hour late!" Rebecca had her hands on her hips, frowning.

Sarah shrugged. "I fell off Racer," she said. "John helped me."

"You fell off Racer?" Rebecca repeated. "Are you hurt?"

Sarah shrugged, again. "I feel well, I think," she said. She handed Racer's reins to John. "Would you be able to take him to the stable for me? It's just around the back."

"Certainly," said John, taking the reins. He looked at her for a moment, then led the horse away.

Rebecca gazed after him. "Who is he?" she whispered. "I don't think I have ever seen him before."

"His name is John Miller," answered Sarah. "He has just moved here with his family."

Rebecca gazed at her, her eyes wide. "And he just happened along, after your fall?"

"*Jah*," Sarah said. "He was out walking. I bumped into him yesterday, as well."

They started walking up the farmhouse steps. "I think that young man likes you, Sarah," Rebecca whispered.

Sarah stopped. "What are you talking about? He just happened along, and was nice enough to assist me."

Rebecca smiled. "I can tell, by the way he looks at you," she said. She narrowed her eyes, looking over her sister. "It's good that you look decent today, even though you had a fall. I have seen you with your hair out, and your *kapps* dislodged. Dirt on your apron. At least you are looking better than usual."

Sarah felt stung. "You are too concerned with appearances, sister," she said, primly. "And as for any interest from that young man, you are imagining it. Besides, I never want to court anyone. I don't want to marry, and get stuck in a farmhouse being a slave, tending to screaming babies forever."

Rebecca looked at her as if she had lost her mind. "There is more to it than that, little sister," she said sharply. "What about love – for your husband, and your children? To serve those you love is a blessing. I couldn't imagine life without my family."

"I'm not criticising you..."

"Enough." Rebecca put a hand in the air to silence her. "You are young, and foolish. I hope that you will see the error of your ways before it is too late, Sarah. For you just might find life passes you by, and suddenly you are a spinster dreaming of what could have been." She walked ahead into the house.

Sarah frowned. Rebecca was just justifying her choices, wasn't she? Not that there were many, really. If you belonged to the community, you always ended up being a wife and mother. Love. Sarah scoffed. Was so called love worth all the nonsense attached to it? Nothing had led her to believe so, thus far.

And yet. She remembered how she had felt, when John had helped her up. The fission of attraction. But what did it matter, anyway? John would prove himself like all the rest of them. Wanting to change her.

Here he was, now. Walking toward her. Her heart started beating faster.

"Sarah." He bowed, his dark eyes shining. She looked at him, awkwardly. What should she say? Should she invite him inside, for a drink? It would probably be polite. After all, he had helped her today.

"Would you like a glass of water, or a coffee?" She blushed, slightly.

"No, no," he said. "I should get going. Chores to do." And yet he stood there, still looking at her.

"Well," Sarah looked at the ground. "Thank you for helping me today. I really appreciated it."

"My pleasure," he said. He looked at her, almost beseechingly. Then he abruptly turned on his heel, and walked away. Back up the track.

Sarah watched him go. She was feeling odd. Was John Miller a friend, or a critic? Was she being judged by him?

She simply didn't know. She only knew that she wanted him to come back. To be by her side. For just a little bit longer.

***

John walked briskly. He was going to be in trouble with his father, again. He didn't even know why he had decided to walk across the plain this morning. He had many chores to do, and his father knew how long each one took. He would be at the farm, now, wondering where on earth John had disappeared to.

He frowned. He was only being half truthful with himself. He knew why he had suddenly decided on the morning walk. He had been hoping to see Sarah again.

He hadn't been able to stop thinking about her. It was as simple as that. He knew that she was considered wild by the community. He knew everyone thought that she wasn't marriage material, that she was too forthright, and reckless. He had seen the evidence of that recklessness, not once, but twice. Yesterday, when she had almost run him down with her horse. And today, when she had fallen from it.

He thought her reckless, like everybody else. And yet, there was something so charismatic about her. The vision of the girl on the horse, hair flying and eyes glittering, was enchanting. And the fact that she had the strength of will to be herself, in the face of disapproval.

But she had admitted it, today. She hated housework, and didn't like babies. How could he sensibly try to court a young woman who had no desire to set up a home and have a family, as was the done thing in their faith? John was a conventional man. He wanted a home and family of his own; he wanted to have children. How could he court a girl who expressed her disdain for both?

He thought of Miriam, the girl he had been courting. Meek Miriam, whose sole desire in life was marriage and children. She was the type of woman he should be considering, not a wild girl like Sarah who flouted convention.

He sighed, deeply. He had better get moving. Sarah would probably not agree to courting him, anyway, with her beliefs. If he suggested it to her, she would probably laugh in his face.

Best to forget all about her. With a nod of decision, John set off towards his farm.

***

The babies were screaming. Sarah had a thudding headache. She didn't know if it was a leftover from her fall today, or just the children. Maybe a combination of both.

Would they ever stop? She had tried everything. Fed them, changed them, tried to get them to sleep. But still, they carried on. She juggled little Eli, the nine-month-old, on her hip, desperately looking down the track to see if Rebecca's buggy was on the way. Samuel, the toddler, had his arms wrapped around her legs, bawling like a banshee.

"Your Mamm will be home soon," she said, in a false cheery voice. "Let's sit on the sofa with a picture book."

She walked into the living room, picking up a book. It was one of her own favorites from childhood. She settled down on the sofa, getting Samuel to crawl up beside her. She kept Eli on her lap.

It was difficult, juggling the book and the baby, but she managed to get it open. And then she started reading.

It was such a sweet story, and she got lost in it, just a little bit. The children quietened down as she read. She could feel Eli's head starting to loll. Samuel snuggled up closer, his eyes riveted onto the book.

As she read the last page, she was amazed to see that Eli had fallen asleep. And Samuel was almost there. He burrowed his head into her side, kissing her.

Her heart melted, just a little bit. She looked at him, being very careful that she didn't disturb Eli.

"Did you like that story, little one?" she whispered. Samuel looked up at her, his big blue eyes shining. He nodded.

"Sa-rah," he said, stringing out her name, as he always did. "I love you."

Sarah gasped. He had never said those words to her, before.

"I love you, too, Samuel," she whispered, leaning over to kiss him on the head. He sighed contentedly, before his eyelids started fluttering and finally closed. He was asleep.

Sarah closed the book. It hadn't been easy, but she had got there. They had settled down. Reading the book had been the trick. Even when they had kept crying, she had continued. Her calm determination had soothed them.

Was that the trick, with babies? Being calm? Not getting upset when they cried?

She knew in her heart that it wasn't always that simple. She had seen Rebecca, the calmest person she knew, sometimes unable to settle them. But it did seem to help. And it made her feel better able to cope with them, if she was feeling calm, instead of stressed and anxious.

And how sweet that moment had been, when little Samuel had told her he loved her.

The front door opened. It was Caleb, Rebecca's husband. She looked at him, raising a finger to her mouth to signal to be quiet. Caleb smiled, walking quietly into the living room.

"Well, well," he whispered. "What do we have here? Well done, Sarah."

Sarah glowed. Usually, whenever Caleb walked into the house when she was looking after the children, it was bedlam. He would have to take over, settling the babies, and Sarah, frazzled, would look for her escape.

They both turned as they heard the buggy pull up outside. And then, Rebecca walked into the room. She raised her eyebrows in amazement at the calm scene in front of her.

"Sarah," she whispered. "What has happened? Where is my hot headed little sister?"

Sarah smiled. Rebecca gently eased Eli out of her arms, carrying him to his cot. Caleb did the same with Samuel, making cooing sounds to the little boy as he stirred in his arms.

Sarah watched her sister and brother-in-law meet in the hallway, after putting their children down. Caleb rested a hand on Rebecca's arm, and she gazed up at him with such a look of love that Sarah gasped.

She had to turn her head away from the tender scene, blinking back tears. Why was she so overcome with emotion? It was inexplicable.

As she said good bye to them, she couldn't resist poking her head into the children's bedrooms, watching them sleep. They looked so precious. Her heart overflowed with love for them.

She rode Racer over the plain, heading home. For once, she listened to the voice in her head that said to not go too fast. She didn't feel the need. And she was half hoping that she might spot John Miller, walking.

But she didn't see him. Why did she feel so disappointed? She barely knew the man, after all.

And he would never deign to court her. Her reputation preceded her, and he was a solemn man. Even though his eyes shone when he beheld her. Sarah shivered, picturing them in her mind.

John's dark eyes followed her all the way home, over the plain.

***

A week passed. Sarah rode out over the plain, but she didn't see him. She tried to tell herself it was for the best. She told herself that he was too solemn for her; they wouldn't have been a good match.

But still, her heart yearned to see him. Her heart would jump when she would see a figure in the distance, her eyes deceiving her. It was him! But it never was. He had obviously decided that she was too hard work.

Today was a magical spring day, a hint of summer in the air. She had ridden Racer a bit, but not too fast. Maybe her fall had made her more cautious, she had no idea. But suddenly, she was aware that her beloved horse could be injured by her recklessness. It just didn't seem worth it, anymore.

She bent down to pick some wildflowers. She thought of the bible passage that she had read last night. It had made her stop and ponder. It was Proverbs 14:16, which said, "One who is wise is cautious and turns away from evil, but a fool is reckless and careless." Had that been her? Had she smashed through life, careless of what was before her? She didn't think that she was a fool. She wanted to be wise.

Suddenly, she looked up. Was it really him, on the horizon? John Miller? Her heart started thumping, uncomfortably.

It was. He walked slowly toward her, his face solemn. And then, he was standing there.

"I thought it was you," he said, his eyes shining. He looked down at the ground, as if he didn't know what to say further.

"John," Sarah said, staring at him. She took a deep breath. It was now, or never.

"*Jah*?" He looked up at her. His face told her all she needed to know.

"I'm sorry," she whispered. "I realise now that I have been reckless. I want to change."

"What?" He looked like he couldn't believe what she had just said.

"Oh, I will probably never be meek," she admitted. "I have a temper. But I have learnt that I should try to control it, and remain calm. I want to be a better person."

He looked at her in amazement. "Sarah," he said. "I love you. For who you are. I wouldn't want you to change. I like that you are different from the other girls." He blushed. "Maybe just tone it down, a little."

"You love me?" she whispered. Her heart overflowed with gladness. "John, I love you, too!"

He stared at her, as if he had never heard such good news. He gently approached her. She gazed up at him, her heart overflowing.

"So, I may court you?" he whispered. "And one day we might marry? Even though you hate housework and don't like babies?"

She laughed, gently. "I mightn't ever like housework," she admitted. "But I know it is a necessary part of life. As for babies – well, maybe one day?" She looked at him, blushing.

He smiled. "Maybe one day," he said. "We can have a long engagement, and wait until you feel you are ready. I don't mind waiting."

Sarah breathed a sigh of relief, and gratitude. It was simply astonishing. A man who was willing to give her the space she needed, and loved her for herself, despite her faults. Who was willing to not listen to everything that he had heard, but simply judge her on what he saw.

That was a man worth keeping. She finally understood what this love thing was all about.

THE END

AN AMISH WINTER

TERRI DOWNES

118

Summer, 1905

The air was finally beginning to clear. Somewhere overhead, a bird began to sing, as though assuring the world it remained unmoved by present circumstances.

"Are you leaving with the others?" Jacob asked.

Mary looked down at her hands, twisted in her lap. "My family want to go," she said.

"I don't blame them," said Jacob. "But do you?"

"How could I stay without them?" asked Mary quietly.

Jacob was silent for a minute.

"You know what I would suggest – what I would ask," he said.

Mary did not reply. She knew.

"I know that, after everything, you may have trouble..." Jacob paused. "Trusting."

Mary leaned back, taking her weight on her hands, feeling the dry grass beneath them. She nodded, as though only to herself. Jacob looked at her, his expression indescribably sad.

"I'm so sorry," he said. "About everything. Everything you've been through. But I hope – I have to hope, and I have to ask now, while I can – "

The bird stopped singing.

"Do you trust me?" he asked. "Could you... trust me?"

***

Two months earlier

"Mary, are you listening?"

"What?"

Mary tilted her head towards her brother, though she did not look up from the furrowed piece of ground that she had been staring at as though she were preparing to interrogate it.

"I said we should be getting at least five bushels per acre," said Paul, waving his arms expansively as he indicated the field before them. "I knew *daed* was on to something with this winter wheat. I bet everyone else is wishing they had joined in when he suggested combining resources for the first year."

"Some of them did," Mary pointed out, scuffling at the ground with the toe of her boot. "The Kauffmans and the Yoders have those few acres on the eastern side, by the windmill. Everyone else is focused on their cattle raising."

"More fool them," said Paul. "If it doesn't rain soon they're going to have problems – meanwhile we're nearly ready to harvest. And the windmill's finished just in time, too."

He nodded to himself. Mary was not sure whether it was her irritable frame of mind causing her to be unfair, but she thought he looked a little smug. He, and their eldest brother Albert, and their father, had all been looking a little too smug ever since they had started construction on that windmill.

They had only arrived in Iowa in September, along with twenty-one other Plain families who had all moved over from Pennsylvania, arriving over the course of a few months. Many had been from their old community. Most of the families had settled themselves with cattle ranges, breeding from the stock they had brought with them across the country. Mary's father had had a different plan. As soon as they had arrived, he had busied himself with buying up vast areas of fertile land and planting it with winter wheat. Albert had expressed his concerns over whether they would be able to plant in time, as they only got everything sorted by the beginning of winter when the temperature was beginning to drop. But a slightly delayed first frost and perfect winter conditions meant that now, coming up to Summer, they were looking forward to a bumper crop of wheat, and did not have to join in the worries of their neighbors over the recent lack of rain.

"Daed was right," reaffirmed Paul happily as they started to make for home, the small white farmstead in the middle of the plain, distinguishable from any other houses within view by the tall shape of the windmill standing near it. "The risk was worth it, all the loans, everything. We'll pay them back in no time."

The loans.

Mary could not help but glance sceptically at her brother as they walked. Did he know? Had her father told him? Or had it been a secret between him and –

"Samuel!" called Paul suddenly.

Mary stopped short, feeling for a moment as though Paul had pulled the name from her head. Then she focused her thoughts and realized that Paul was waving at two figures cutting across the pasture to their right.

"Jacob!"

Paul waved at the two men as they approached. He sent a smile in Mary's direction, which Mary felt herself obliged to return. He would of course expect her to be pleased to see Samuel, and she did not want to give her feelings away. Not yet.

"Evening," said Samuel, as he and Jacob came onto the path alongside Mary and Paul.

Jacob smiled in greeting. He and Samuel, both young and unmarried, had become good friends on the long journey to Iowa, and now went nearly everywhere together. One might have thought they were brothers, if not for the fact that they looked nothing alike. Where Samuel was fair, with corn colored hair and light blue eyes, Jacob's complexion was muddy, his hair a dingy red.Where Samuel was strong and well-built, Jacob was lean, looking as though he had grown too tall for his strength. He carried himself as though he had just woken up, as though he were waiting to stretch.

Samuel had been the most handsome man Mary had ever met, she had known so as soon as she had seen him at their first gathering before the big move. His bearing and manner seemed to carry the assumption that people would look at him – but he had looked at Mary, at that first meeting, and smiled.

He was smiling now. Mary looked away.

She was determined to act normally, but she was having trouble collecting her wits as Samuel fell into step alongside her. As though they were already engaged, as though everything had been settled. She felt him looking at her – could he tell that she knew?

"I haven't seen you in a few days," he said, softly enough that it was obvious he was speaking only to her, but loud enough that the others could hear. Mary blushed. He really was being far too obvious – wasn't he? Maybe they did things differently in his old community, but in hers, courtships were quiet things.

"Did you two know how well the wheat is doing?" she said, deliberately catching Paul's eye and smiling as she spoke, which she knew would set him off. It did.

"Oh yes," he said excitedly. "Five bushels an acre at least!"

He started explaining the plans they had for harvest, and how they had been working to get the mill ready so they could grind the flour themselves.

"Will you be selling us your crop to grind, Jacob?" he asked. Jacob's family, the Yoders, had been one of the only two families to take Mary's father up on his offer of land and seeds. They had only planted a couple of acres, on the edge of the land Mary's father had bought, but they would surely benefit from the success of the wheat.

Jacob smiled in that way he had, as though he was thinking of something privately funny. "Maybe," he said. "I wasn't sure whether I should keep the whole crop or burn some of it so I can use the space for corn."

"Corn?" exclaimed Paul, with the attitude of a man who had been farming for decades and knew everything there was to know about the subject. "You'd need a miracle to grow corn in this weather. You're much better off keeping the wheat and letting us grind it. The windmill's nearly done, you know."

Mary was starting to feel embarrassed. As pleased as she had been to find their family settled and prospering so soon, this attitude of her brothers and father seemed too close to pride to allow her much comfort.

"I heard," Jacob was saying.

"We were actually headed over to take a look if we could," said Samuel.

Paul nodded, and seemed about to launch into a description of the brand new windmill, but Mary spoke first.

"You can't," she said.

The boys all glanced at her.

"Why not?" demanded Paul.

"It's getting dark."

"What's that got to do with anything?"

"Weren't you listening to *daed*?" Mary felt her tone becoming sharp, and tried to sound more indulgent. "You can't take a candle or a lantern into the mill."

"Oh, right..." Paul looked a little crestfallen.

"Why?" asked Jacob, still smiling.

"It's the flour dust in the air," explained Mary. "It can catch fire."

"Flour catches fire?" he said, sounding intrigued. "I didn't know that."

"Not by itself so much, not when it's in a sack or a bowl. It's only when it's floating in the air, I think because the fire can get to all the little pieces individually..."

"I never knew," said Jacob. "Did you know that, Samuel?"

"Of course," said Samuel, who had been giving sidelong glances to Mary as she had been speaking. Rather than expounding on the topic, however, he changed the subject.

Mary was again unsure of whether she was simply in a more suspicious frame of mind than usual, but she was certain, as she looked at Samuel, that he had not known. That he was lying to seem clever.

This was going to be a problem, she realized. How could she go courting with a man whom she could not trust?

And even Jacob and Paul, walking along and listening to Samuel – Mary kept looking at them, and wondering – *did you know, too? How many people knew about this before I did?*

Mary clenched and unclenched her fists as they walked. Something would need to be done.

***

"How did you find out?" asked Mary's mother, her brow creased.

"Mrs. Yoder mentioned it," said Mary. "In passing. Though – forgive me – but I can't see that that's the most important point here. When were *you* going to tell me?"

Mary's mother hesitated, and glanced at her father. He was standing at the window of their front room, staring out across the yard and the space beyond, towards his new windmill.

"We – well, we thought – " began her mother.

"We thought we would wait until you had had a chance to get to know Samuel," said her father, turning from the window and facing his daughter. His expression was calm and earnest. "You were getting on so well with him, we thought it might make you uncomfortable to know that he was the one who lent us the wheat money."

Mary frowned a little, turning this over in her mind.

"Yes," she said, "but *he* knew that he had lent the money. He had information I didn't..."

"Goodness, Mary, you're not negotiating a business deal," laughed her father.

"It's not as though *you* owe him anything," said her mother.

"Yes, I know that..." said Mary slowly, hesitating.

She was having trouble remembering her original objections. She had been deeply shocked when Jacob's mother had casually referred to the loan Samuel had given to her father, the one that had allowed him to get the crop planted in time, the success of which had then enabled him to secure a second loan for the construction of the windmill.

She had immediately thought back to the way that Samuel had approached her that night he had first invited her out for a drive. He had been smiling, the way he always did, with that calm assurance that she had so often admired. But had he been so assured because he felt that she did, in fact, owe him something for her family's success?

There were so many questions she wanted to ask. When had her father first asked Samuel about the loan? Had it been before or after Samuel had started smiling at Mary, seeking her out and engaging her in conversation? Had it been Samuel's idea not to tell Mary, or her father's?

And had her parents' encouragement of her courtship with Samuel been because they thought the two of them were well suited, or because they felt obliged to the man?

But now, looking at the reassuring smile her father was showing her, Mary could not bring herself to ask. It might sound as though she was accusing them of – what?

So she nodded. "I understand," she said. "I just feel foolish, acting in ignorance."

"We're sorry that you feel that way," her father said kindly. "It wasn't our intention."

Mary told him that she understood, and agreed that they would not mention her knowledge to Samuel just yet. Then she excused herself, saying that she had to see to her chores.

When she walked outside into the front yard, she found her gaze drawn to the windmill. It soared up against the sky, its four sailcloths giving the unsettling impression of outstretched arms. With the sun setting behind it, all she could see was its shape in shadow.

***

Mary could not think of a real reason why she should drop her courtship with Samuel. The points her father had made were sensible, and the liking she had felt for Samuel was genuine. Perhaps secrecy really had been the best thing, she considered, else she might have been confused as to whether her feeling had sprung from gratitude or from real admiration.

Yet, she found herself avoiding Samuel. Not entirely – they still went for rides, and walks. But she never asked when they would see each other again. She never pushed for extra time together, or told him that she had missed him.

He did not seem to notice the change. Mary tried to convince herself that this was simply because he was confident that she liked him, and not because he did not care whether she did or not. She tried not to count the number of times he actually asked for her opinion.

She spent the afternoons before their scheduled drives going over potential topics of conversation, trying to talk herself into feeling more comfortable than she did by pre-planning the time they would have together.

On one such afternoon, as the sun was sinking over the wide plains in a haze of orange, she was so far gone in her thoughts as she completed her chores in readiness for her evening out that she failed to notice Jacob approaching across the back yard until he was level with the porch. When she saw his long sunset-cast shadow fall across the steps she jumped, sending a puff of flour into the air.

"It's only me," said Jacob, holding his hands up in front of him, his shoulders in their slightly relaxed slouch like always. "Are you all right?"

"Fine," said Mary, placing a hand to her heart, then pulling it away and glancing down in irritation when she saw that she had smeared flour on the neck of her dress.

Jacob watched her, one side of his mouth quirked in a partial smile. Mary shook her head at her thoughtlessness and smiled back.

Something about the openness of his expression made her feel more calm than she had in weeks – since learning of the loan.

"I'm just here to arrange getting my grain milled," said Jacob, walking up the steps. "Your father's agreed to buy my crop. Seems funny, seeing as how I bought the seeds from him in the first place, but we'll all profit in the end, I'm sure."

"You're not going to try corn, then?" asked Mary.

"Not with the weather the way it is."

They had had barely any rain in the last month, and the almanacs were predicting a very dry summer.

"Maybe you could try next year," said Mary. "Or you could alternate the wheat with a legume crop."

"That's a good idea," said Jacob thoughtfully. "And I'm trying to think of ways around the water problem."

"Like what?" asked Mary. It felt good, she realized, to be speaking like this. Discussing important, practical things, things that would reward you for the thought you put into them, instead of winding your concentration around ideas like love and betrayal and gratitude.

"Irrigation, maybe. There's a brook running alongside the my land, between mine and the Kauffman's, you know, and I thought I could use it for the fields. It's still flowing, even without the rain."

"I know the one you mean," said Mary. "I think it's ground water, from a spring, so you don't have to worry about the rain. Will the Kauffmans do the same on their side?"

"John's still ill," said Jacob, shaking his head. "And the oldest boys are having trouble handling things on their own."

"Perhaps you could do it for them," said Mary.

Jacob considered this, and smiled. "Of course," he said. "I should have thought of that."

"I'm sure you would have," Mary assured him. Although she wanted to keep talking, she knew that Samuel would be coming by soon, so she turned her attention back to the table in front of her.

"What are you doing?" asked Jacob, not moving.

"Kneading dough," said Mary, raising an eyebrow.

Jacob laughed. "No, I can see that, I just wondered why you were doing it out here on the porch."

"It gets too hot in the kitchen at this time," shrugged Mary. "We still need to put up shutters to block the afternoon light, but the boys are all busy getting ready for the harvest."

"Ah. I thought you might be using the sunlight instead of a lamp in case you set fire to the flour," he teased.

Mary rolled her eyes. "Only if you throw the flour over the lamp," she said.

"I'll have to try that sometime," Jacob said. "I keep trying to imagine what you were describing, but it's difficult."

"Hmm..." Mary glanced at her kneading. She was just about done. "Hold on."

She went back into the kitchen and came out with a candle in a holder, along with a bowl of water. She handed Jacob the bowl, then set the candle on the far end of the table and lit it.

"Right," she said. "This looks better at night, but for once there's no breeze, so I might as well show you now. Have the water ready in case I make a mistake."

Jacob nodded eagerly, looking for all the world like a schoolboy. Mary could not help but smile at his expression. She took a small handful of flour, then stood at arm's length away from the candle and cast the flour carefully over the flame.

A ball of fire blossomed out from the candle, reaching up and engulfing the falling flour in a flash of light which disappeared into a wisp of yellow flame.

It lasted only a second, but left an after image of light burning in Mary's eyes, forming a bright haze around Jacob's face as she looked up at him to gauge his expression. He looked completely entranced.

"That was amazing! Can we do it again?"

"One's enough," said Mary. "Getting overexcited is how accidents happen."

"All right," he said reluctantly. "Then – "

"What are you doing?" a voice called from across the yard.

Mary and Jacob turned to see Samuel striding toward them. He did not look pleased.

"I was just showing Jacob how the fire reacts with the flour..." began Mary, but she trailed off as Samuel's face remained set in a scowl.

"I asked to see," said Jacob, keeping his voice light. He glanced at Mary. As she met his gaze, she shook her head slightly, indicating that he did not need to stay and defend her. He hesitated for a moment, then said, "Well, I'd best catch your father before he heads off."

Jacob disappeared into the house. Mary tried to smile at Samuel, but she was thrown by his still-angry expression.

***

The next day, Mary sought out her parents once more. She had spent half the night thinking about the decision she had to make, but it was getting harder and harder to ignore the way her heart was turning.

She felt as though she had been caught up, off her feet, for the months she and Samuel had been courting. Caught up by his good looks, by his confidence, by the fact that he seemed to favor her over any other girl in their new community. Even the fact that he had come from a different community within Lancaster had added to his appeal; unlike young men such as Jacob, Mary had not ever known Samuel as a boy, but only as a man.

It had taken the shock of finding out about the loan to shake her from her trance. She had started having doubts – and then, with her newly opened eyes, finding more things to doubt about. She had started to notice how little they ever spoke about her, the two of them. It was always Samuel leading the conversation, and Mary trying to show him how interested she was.

And yesterday... he had gone on about her candle trick for almost half of the buggy ride they had taken. "It's not safe, you were just showing off, think about how you'd behave if you were running a home," and on and on.

Mary had tried to explain that she had done it before, and had even apologized, admitting that it had not been the most sensible thing to do. But he had not let up. And eventually, Mary had started to wonder... was it what she had done that had annoyed him? Or the fact that she had done it for Jacob?

She had thought about how happy Jacob always was to see her, how he sought her smiles and opinion... how friendly they had been back in Lancaster, and how she barely saw him these days, since she had been seeing Samuel. And she had wondered.

She left this latter concern unspoken to her parents, as she could not be sure of Jacob's feelings for her, or Samuel's feelings about those feelings, but she explained that she had misgivings about Samuel's character.

She had been nervous about broaching the subject, as her parents had both been so pleased by Samuel's courtship, but they both sat and listened to her speak without interrupting. In fact, Mary watched her father nodding thoughtfully and began to think how good it was of him not to object to this, given what he owed Samuel and how careful he was bound to be not to offend him. She was going to say as much – but her father spoke first.

"Now, Mary... are you sure that you are not reacting too strongly?" he asked.

Mary looked at him.

"You don't want to make a mistake," he said. "Are you sure you've thought this through?"

His voice was calm, his expression kind. His eyebrows were raised.

As though he knew better than her. As thought he knew that she was simply being over emotional, and that she did not know her own mind.

Mary felt something cold spreading at the bottom of her chest.

"I'm quite sure," she said, keeping her voice steady, even as fear began to make itself known. He could not have misunderstood what she had been saying. So why was he questioning her?

He had always trusted her in the past. Always. He knew that she respected his authority, and had never challenged her unnecessarily over the fact. He had always told her how proud he was of her intelligence, and how she could work things out on her own.

Surely he would not...

But he did.

"Well, I would rather you allowed Samuel to go on courting you," he said. "For now. Something might change, you know. You might realize you were wrong."

Mary spoke quietly. "I don't think I will, *daed*."

Her father's expression closed. "Well, I want you to try," he said. And nodded, sharply. And then left the room.

Mary turned to her mother – who was already turning away.

"*Mamme*?" she said.

"Trust your *daed*," her mother said. "He knows what's best."

Mary left the room without another word.

***

"What's the problem?" asked Albert. "If you don't like him, break it off."

He grabbed the side of the bin in front of him and gave it a shake. "This one's secure!" he called up to Paul on the next floor. "Try the hopper."

"Which one's the hopper?" Paul yelled down.

"Where you put the grain in," Albert yelled back. "You'd think with how excited he is about this, he'd remember what everything's called," he commented to Mary.

He and Paul were double checking the workings of the windmill before they started the harvest. They had already checked the sailcloths; the shafts, pinions and spindles; and the two huge stone millwheels.

"That's what I wanted to do," said Mary, "but *daed* thinks I'm making a mistake."

She did not tell him the shadowed suspicions in her heart, that their father was insisting she keep Samuel happy because of what they owed him. She did not want to sully her father's image in the eyes of his sons; nor, indeed, did she want Albert to become angry at her for suggesting such a thing.

"Hopper's fine," said Paul, as his feet appeared on the ladder above their heads.

"Well then, either you're wrong or *daed's* wrong," said Albert.

He led the way back outside, into bright sunshine that made Mary squint. The sun was still relentless, the sky obstinately blue, the air baked to a crisp every single morning. Many of the families in the area were beginning to wonder what they would do if the rain continued to stay away,

"Right," said Paul, following them out. "You'll find out soon enough."

He looked back up at the windmill. "A lot of people are going to be buying our flour," he said. "Especially now they haven't been able to plant much themselves."

"It's a shame," said Albert, not sounding too concerned. "It's turning into a real drought now, I don't know how everyone's going to manage. I think we'll be the only ones around here who'll have had any success this year."

Mary felt herself becoming desperate. If only they were not all so caught up in this wretched windmill business. She could not remember any of her family being so distant and unfeeling as this before. She was beginning to wish that they had never even come here, that they had just stayed home in Lancaster. All this talk of crop yields and profits... it felt so wordly. Even though the windmill was approved technology, her father and brothers were so obsessed with the thing that Mary felt that they might as well have gone and bought one of those new motorcar things that everyone seemed to have had in the towns that they had passed through on their way here.

"Listen. It's just that I think *daed*... likes Samuel too much," she pressed on. "As a... friend. And I think he might not realize that were not suited."

Albert dragged his gaze away from the sailcloths, which were currently immobile as the mechanisms were all in place now and should not be turned when there was nothing to grind.

"And what do you want us to do about it?" he asked, as though conceding a huge favor.

Mary swallowed down her irritation. "Just... there are a few people who knew Samuel, from his community, back in Lancaster," she said. "Who knew his family. You're all working together in the harvest – just, if you could ask them, in passing, what they think of Samuel. What they know of him. Something."

Albert sighed. Mary turned to Paul. "Please," she repeated, hoping her younger brother would be a little softer.

Paul looked at Albert. "I don't mind," he said.

Mary took that as a yes.

***

She left things at that, for a little while. She did not have to think too much about seeing Samuel, or indeed her father or brothers, as they were all busy dawn til dusk with the harvest. And she kept herself as busy as possible, so that at least half the times Samuel tried to see her she could tell him that she was in the middle of something.

As the days passed, the ground remained dry, the plains wide and brown under the sun as though they had been scorched by it. The cattle farmers were beginning to become seriously worried. Some even began to speak of returning to Lancaster. Mary's father greeted this news with annoyance, and Mary could not help the uncharitable thought that he was angry not because he might lose his community, but because he might lose his customers.

She repented of the thought after she had had it, but it left its shadow behind.

When Samuel mentioned to her, one evening, that he had also been considering whether staying was the right option, Mary almost panicked, thinking that he meant to propose, that he wanted them to wed and return to Lancaster together. She quickly began to speak of the last dry summer she had experienced, when she was seven, and how everyone had felt then, but that the rain had come anyway, and that if they just remained faithful in prayer –

She realized, as she spoke, that Samuel was not really paying attention. She did not mind, as she was just trying to keep the subject changed. They were walking back to her home, and had almost reached the yard gate, and soon she could say good night.

As they reached the gate, she turned to say goodnight, hoping to cut off any ideas of him coming inside with her. But as she did so, she caught sight of something.

"Oh, look!" she cried excitedly, and pointed.

Over the long line of the horizon, a cloud was rising. Just one, by itself, but it was no wisp that would blow away in the night. It was large, substantial, and heavy, with a darkness underneath the pink caused by the setting sun that hinted at the possibility of rain. Rain, at last.

"It's a cloud!"

"I can see that," said Samuel, sounding a little amused.

Mary ignored him, looking out at the cloud with as much satisfaction as if she had made it herself. She hardly noticed Samuel beside her, looking away from it.

But then he glanced down at her. And as she reached out to open the gate, he reached out to stop her, placing a hand on the latch. And the other hand on the small of her back.

Mary felt a jolt up her spine, and stepped away with a jerk, turning so that her back was to the gate. She stared at Samuel. He looked quite calm – had she made a mistake? But he reached out again, to her shoulder, and ran his hand down to her elbow. His expression was soft, a smile playing on his lips. Mary almost wondered if her reaction was unwarranted.

But he was not – he was not supposed to do this. He was not allowed. Mary took a deep breath. Whether his old community had different rules or not – and, really, how different could they be, now that she thought about it – she had not given him permission to do this. They were not engaged. They were not married. He had no right to touch her.

She pulled her arm away. Samuel raised an eyebrow. It looked like a challenge.

What can I say? Mary wondered. *What can I say to make him leave? Please, please, leave –*

And then she heard them. Footsteps. Louder than they should have been, on the dust of the road, or perhaps that was because Mary was so happy to hear them.

"Jacob," she said, unable to keep the relief from her voice. She caught Samuel's frown, but did not care, as Jacob approached with his easy smile.

"Evening," he said, but Samuel was already turning around.

"Evening," he replied. "I have to go."

"Oh, all right – " Jacob hesitated as he found himself speaking to his friend's receding back.

It may have been Mary's imagination, but she thought she saw a flicker of something, as Jacob watched Samuel leave. Something cold. Something hard.

He turned to Mary, his face creasing as he apparently noticed her distress.

"What's wrong?"

"Nothing," said Mary. Lying. She swallowed. "How have you been? Have you managed your irrigation project yet?"

Jacob nodded, still looking as though he wanted to press her for details. But she smiled encouragingly, and he began explaining the work he had done on his and his neighbor's fields.

"It worked so well that I did end up burning some of the wheat so I could plant other things there," he said, leaning his forearms along the top of the gate and craning his head forward to see past the windmill to their right. "Vegetables and so on, things that can grow in the fall."

"Was that this week? I wondered what the smoke was," said Mary.

"I did it in sections, keeping it under control, you know," said Jacob. "I remembered your candle demonstration, I didn't want to risk the windmill going up."

He smiled. And Mary felt the warmth of knowing that he had acknowledged her input. That he was showing her he respected her.

And that he wanted respect in return. Why else would he have come to tell her that he had done as she said and helped his neighbors? He had no other reason to come over.

Mary found herself smiling back. She knew, now, after this evening, that she could never be with Samuel. And when that was done, then who knew? Maybe Jacob...

"Do you know what was wrong with Samuel?" Jacob was asking.

"We just... had a disagreement," said Mary carefully, leaning against the gatepost and looking out at the darkening sky. "Things are a little strained."

"Right..." Jacob glanced toward the house. "Is that..." he stopped.

"Is that what?" asked Mary.

"I was wondering. Um..."

Mary began to feel worried. Jacob was not meeting her eyes. "What is it? Tell me."

"I don't want to overstep," he said, still looking away. "I thought maybe your father had already cleared everything up, when I saw you with Samuel. But then, if you're unhappy about it all – "

"What all?" asked Mary. He was not making any sense.

He looked up, then. Surprised.

"The... you know, about Samuel?" he coughed. "Your brothers were asking around, and one of the men – you know, Eli Miller, he said he had heard a rumor a while back, and he didn't want to spread it but if they were worried..." he trailed off.

Mary was still staring.

"They told your father," he said. "A few days ago. Did he not tell you?"

"No." Mary stepped toward Jacob so she could look him right in the eye, through the settling darkness. "Tell me."

Jacob swallowed. And he told her.

And Mary felt her insides turn to ice.

***

"You don't understand."

"Obviously not," said Mary, her throat tight. "I'm asking you to explain it to me."

They all looked upset. Her father, Paul, Albert. No, not even upset – annoyed. Annoyed that Mary had called them from their work and was pestering them with questions when they had better things to do.

"If there had been any substance to that rumor," her father said through gritted teeth, glancing out through the front window, "of course we would have told you. But we saw no reason to upset you with something that might just be lies."

"But it might have been true," hissed Mary.

Outside, the sky was low and gray, the cloud from the evening before having been joined by a mass of others. There had been no rain, but there was a warm wind gusting hard across the fields, whipping the grass into long, snaking waves.

The men her father had helping him put the grain through the mill would be working frantically to keep up the pace, Mary thought. And her father and brothers obviously wanted to join them. But they had not gone yet. And she knew – she knew, somehow – that this meant they had been caught out. If they truly believed there was nothing to worry about then they would have gone back out to work.

"But that girl wasn't pregnant," Albert pointed out, his mouth twisting distastefully as he said the words. "Obviously."

"She might have lost it," Paul said quietly, though the other two glared at him for this.

"Whether she was or not," said Mary, "the fact that there was reason to think she might have been speaks for itself."

"She might have been lying," said her father.

"Why on earth would she lie about that?" Mary snapped, just managing to stop herself from shouting the words.

She glanced at the door, wishing she had waited for her mother to return from the Yoders' before starting this conversation. Surely she would have understood. But then, would she not have been told the story along with her father? Would she not also have chosen to ignore it?

A low rumble of thunder shook the house. Mary felt herself anticipating the tapping of raindrops on the windowpanes, but none followed. Just more dry wind, more waiting, more frustration.

"We don't know any of these people, from Samuel's old community," her father pointed out. In his calm, collected manner. "We had no reason to think badly of Samuel. Why would we believe such a rumor without proof?"

"I believe it," Mary said.

That, finally, got her father's full attention. Her brothers also looked away from the frantically turning windmill, their expressions matched in horror.

"Mary – you didn't – you and Samuel – "

"What? No," Mary said, shocked in her turn. "*No.*"

"Then why would you – "

"It wasn't – I mean, there were moments." Mary closed her eyes briefly. "When I could tell. If I had let him, he would have."

It had not just been that touch, last night.

It had been in the way he looked at her. His eyes raking her up and down, stopping where they should not. The way he had sought her away from everyone else, the way he blocked her when there were other people present. The way he treated her as though she were already his.

She had chosen not to notice. She had not wanted to.

"How could you not tell me?" she asked quietly.

And then, because if she was ever going to feel justified in asking this question, it was now:

"Was it because of the money?"

And her father would not look at her.

"Was it worth it?" she asked, her voice almost a whisper.

"The windmill," she heard Albert say.

She covered her face with her hands. "Stop it."

"No, the windmill – "

"*I don't care about the – *"

"No, look!"

Albert was pointing, frozen, his face the color of ash. Pointing outside. Across the yard, and the pasture beyond, to the windmill. To the men running away from it. To the thin, dark stream of smoke rising above.

*****

"I wondered where you were."

Mary looked up, shielding her eyes, even though the sky was still purpled with clouds. They were still irritated from the smoke, as were the insides of her nose and throat, and she did not want to open them at all. But she managed to smile at Jacob, who looked even worse than she did. He sat down next to her and took off his shoes as she had, joining her as she dangled her feet in the stream. His stream.

He had come running, yesterday. She had seen him from the back pasture, where she had run to with her family once they had realized that they would not be able to put the fire out. Paul and Albert had had to forcibly drag their father away to stop him from trying to get back and save his beloved windmill.

They had run until they heard the explosion of flames behind them which signaled that the flour-filled air inside of the mill had caught. Mary had glimpsed it from the corner of her eye as she had looked behind her; a sudden rush and roar of brightness leaping into the sky.

They had watched as the structure had been eaten away, blackening and crumbling. The fire had spread to the sailcloths, which continued to whip themselves around in the wind, billowing flames and smoke in their wake, flinging burning debris as far as it would go. Onto the dry grass of the next pasture. Into what was left of the wheat fields. Onto the house.

And Jacob had come running, sprinting toward the fire. Dragging them back with him, as the fire and smoke followed them across the dry fields. Back to his home. The only safe place – because, as he had told Mary, he had, just that week, burned a large strip of his land to prepare it for planting. And fire will not burn across something that has been burned already.

Mary's mother had met them as they arrived, her eyes wild with fear. They had stayed standing outside the house, catching their breath, coughing, watching in the distance as everything they owned turned to ash, praying for the rain to start. But the clouds had remained obstinate and aloof, and the fire had continued its path until it petered out at the edges of the wheat fields.

"Have they found out what caused it yet?" Mary asked now.

Jacob shrugged, and covered a cough. He and the others had used the water from his spring to dampen the ground around his house, just in case, and he had had to spend a lot of time in the way of the wind-driven smoke. His skin still looked a little gray, and Mary could smell that he was several baths away from ridding himself of the odor.

"Might have been lightning," he said. "Or the speed of the wind. If there was a piece in the mechanism that hadn't been properly oiled, it could have sparked."

Mary nodded. "To be honest," she said, "I don't really care. And – and I'm glad its gone."

She wondered if she would have to explain herself, but Jacob was nodding. Someone – probably Paul, she thought – had filled him in. On everything.

"I'm sorry for your family's losses," he said, "but honestly – me too."

They paddled their feet for another minute. The air was finally beginning to clear. Somewhere overhead, a bird began to sing, as though assuring the world it remained unmoved by present circumstances.

"Are you leaving with the others?" Jacob asked.

This morning, there had been an emergency meeting called. All the families. There had been talk already of leaving, of heading back to Lancaster. There was no blessing here, some had said. Even if there was rain, now, it would be such hard work to keep going. It was too much. They were ready to leave.

Others had wanted to stay. Jacob's fields had been saved, as had the Kauffman's. A few other families seemed on the fence, each seeming to want someone else to make a firm commitment before they followed. There were five in all. Not that many. But enough for a start.

Mary looked down at her hands, twisted in her lap. "My family want to go," she said.

"I don't blame them," said Jacob. "But do you?"

"How could I stay without them?" asked Mary quietly.

Jacob was silent for a minute.

"You know what I would suggest – what I would ask," he said.

Mary did not reply. She knew. Hers had been the first name he had called, as he had run to them the day before. Hers had been the hand he had held, pulling her to safety. She was the one he had come to, over the course of the afternoon, to check on. To reassure.

There was no hiding it now.

"I know that, after everything, you may have trouble..." Jacob paused. "Trusting."

Mary leaned back, taking her weight on her hands, feeling the dry grass beneath them. She nodded, as though only to herself. Jacob looked at her, his expression indescribably sad.

"I'm so sorry," he said. "About everything. Everything you've been through. But I hope – I have to hope, and I have to ask now, while I can – "

The bird stopped singing.

"Do you trust me?" he asked. "Could you... trust me?"

Mary closed her eyes. She thought about her father. Her brothers. Samuel. The men who she had trusted before.

And then she thought of Jacob. Showing her such care and kindness even when he thought they she could never be his.

And, on her smoke-singed, upturned face, she felt it. The first fat, wet raindrop, hitting her so hard she could hear it against her skin. And another. And another.

The bird flew off, presumably excited about the prospect of worms. And Mary and Jacob stayed where they were. The rain fell harder, and Mary blinked drops off her eyelashes. She caught Jacob looking at her. And smiled.

"Yes," she said. "I do."

MY CHRISTIAN COWBOY

JENNIFER ANN RAMSEY

Chapter One: The Meeting

Bill sat on the porch of his mother's small farm home shining his boots. Bill took pride of his things, and these boots had to last him for the whole season. It was hard to keep boots clean in his line of work.

Bill grew up with his mother in a small town in Missouri. She had lived there since Bill was born over twenty-two years ago. His job took him out west, though. He was a bounty hunter. When someone would break the law, he would go after them and pick them up. When he brought the criminal to the sheriff, he would get a reward. The land wasn't very developed, and most criminals decided to hide out west. Bill worked especially hard to get the job done, which helped develop quite the reputation. Bill needed to catch every criminal he could to get paid. After his father died, his mother was left alone. Bill felt the need to support her. Bill's mother, Annie, didn't exactly like her son's career, but she had to admit that he was good at it.

Annie was starting to wear the wisdom and pain of old age. Her hair was more gray than blonde, and she had wrinkles under her eyes. She was usually seen smiling, though, especially when her son was safe and at home with her. She was known around the small town for her feisty attitude, her cooking, and her talent for making clothes.

"Finish up and come get some of this chili, boy," Annie called out to her son.

"I'm almost done, ma!"

"Well, I don't want to hear a word when your chili is cold."

"Is there cornbread?"

"You ungrateful boy, you better get in here and take what you're given before you get nothing!"

Bill put down his polish and boots and headed into the wooden home. The home was small, but it had a comfortable feeling about it. On the table, next to the kitchen, were two bowls of chili (and cornbread).

"This looks great, ma!" Bill said, sitting down on the bench.

"You are not thinking of having supper before washing up, are you?"

"I'm fine, ma! All I did was go out into town today and get shoe polish."

"You will not sit at my table without washing up. Wash your hands and your face."

Bill obeyed. He spent his days chasing dangerous criminals around the country, but he was still afraid of his mother's whippings.

"So, how long are you staying this time?"

Bill always hated this question. She made him feel guilty, but he had to leave to bring money home. "Sheriff Lawrence told me that he has a job for me. I'm planning on heading there in the morning."

"But you just came home yesterday!"

"I know. I gotta get more money when I can, though. You hardly have any flour left. You have no sugar. I'm glad I came home when I did., but the money that I brought home will only last for so long."

"You know I worry about you when you're not here."

"Just keep busy with church and cooking and your dresses. You won't even know I was gone."

"You know I worry."

Bill saved his cornbread for last. He dipped it in the remainder of the chili in his bowl and took a big bite. "I am gonna miss your cornbread."

After dinner, Annie did the dishes and read the Bible before bed while Bill finished polishing his boots and drank some of his moonshine.

The sun woke Bill up the next morning bright and early. Annie was already up doing her daily chores. Bill went out to feed his horse, Bonnie, and get ready for his next job.

"I suppose I'll see you again in another month or so."

"That depends on how long the job takes me, ma."

"Well, I love you. Be good. I packed you some food to take with you."

With that, Bill got ready for his next job. He rode down to the sheriff's station, and he tied Bonnie up before getting inside. Sheriff O'Malley was a beast of a man. His large stature alone helped to keep order in the area. He also had a large gun that helped.

"Well, there's the top bounty hunter in the whole West looking for another bounty I reckon."

"Well, I need to keep my ma in those nice dress that she makes."

"You know, I've been meaning to tell the wife that it's about time for her to get another Sunday dress. Between you and me, hers is starting to look a little ragged."

"I'm surprised you're willing to spend the money."

"Lord knows I don't want to."

"Well, what have you got for me, Sheriff?"

"To be honest, you've been rounding them up pretty good. We don't have too much right now."

"Come on. You know I gotta work."

"Well, there is one thing, but I'm not sure you'll take it. The Thompsons down in Independence were asking for some help with their daughter. Apparently, they haven't seen her in some time. They will be willing to pay you. They have some money."

"I guess if that's what I need to do then that's what I need to do. I'll head that way right now."

Independence was a bit of a distance, but Bill was sure that she could get there before dinner. He rode throughout the day, only to stop for water a couple of times. When he got to Independence, he stopped at the general store to get some whiskey and some candies. He was also able to ask the person behind the counter to tell him how to get to the Thompson home. He learned that Mr. Thompson was the local pastor, and t he house was just up the road about half a mile.

As Bill came up to the gorgeous but modest house with blue shutters and horses in the back, he saw another site that caught his eye: a young woman in a simple skirt, blouse, and boots. Her hair was in a long, messy braid, and she had the most beautiful smile that Bill had ever seen.

Chapter Two: Katy Thompson and Family

"Excuse me, ma'am. Can you tell me if this is the Thompson residence?"

"I sure can. Katy Thompson. Pleasure to meet you. What brings you around? I haven't seen you here before." The girl spoke with elegance and had a flair of sophistication to her demeanor. Her clothes didn't look especially fancy, but it wasn't Sunday. She also smelled of horses and flowers.

"I'm a bounty hunter and Sheriff O'Malley sent me. I understand that you may need some assistance finding someone.

Katy's eyes lit up. "Oh, come this way. My folks will be so happy to see you. They have been worried sick. Here, let your horse in back with the others. She's not too mean, is she? I don't want her scaring my horse."

"Nope. She's a gentle giant. She'll be just fine."

Katy was moving quickly. "I am so happy that you're here!"

Bill followed the beautiful girl into the family home. The house smelled like cherry pie, and Bill was suddenly painfully aware of how hungry he was.

"Mama! Papa! This man here says he wants to help find Lizzie."

The small family gathered into the main room quickly. Bill could feel the hope in the air the way that the family was so excited.

"Please! Come in. What's your name?"

"Do you know where Lizzie is?

"Are you hungry? Can I get you something to eat? Take off your boots. You're our guest."

When they finally stopped talking, Bill sat down and slowly took off his boots. He could feel the eyes on him.

"My name is Bill. I'm a bounty hunter by trade, and my local sheriff said that you were looking for help. I'm his number one bounty hunter, and I have a very good success rate."

"She's not a criminal or anything," Mr. Thompson said quickly. "She's just always been a little wild. She was always a good girl. She would help me at church every Sunday. It wasn't until recently that she started misbehaving."

"What was she doing to misbehave?"

"Well, she started dating a boy. I told her that I disapproved, but she wasn't going to let that stop her. I often wish that I had just let her date him. Maybe she would still be with us if I had," said Mrs. Thompson.

"Don't blame yourself, mama."

"And you guys have no idea where she might have gone?" Bill asked.

"She probably left with her boyfriend to Shadow Creek. The only problem is that it is quite far away in Kansas," said Katy. "Her boyfriend had family there."

"I simply can't abandon my congregation. They need me."

Bill nodded. "Well, I am happy to go travel down there and bring her back for you. That's no problem."

"Oh, thank you! We will pay you. We will pay you everything that we have. We just want our little girl back," said Mrs. Thompson.

"I will only need a couple of supplies and a small advance. When I return with Lizzie, we can complete the payment," said Bill. "I'll leave tomorrow. Now, as the first part of the payment, do you think that I can have some of whatever smells so darn delicious around here?"

"Yes! Yes! Yes! Katy, go whip him up a plate."

"Absolutely, mama."

"We will have to send the sheriff our thanks for sending you to us. You are the answer to our prayers," said Mr. Thompson.

"Well," said Bill," I appreciate it, but don't thank me too much yet. You can thank me when I come back with your daughter. And maybe I can enjoy one of your sermons then."

"Oh, that would be wonderful. You will be my special guest," said Mr. Thompson.

"What happens if she says she doesn't want to come back?" Katy asked putting a plate in front of Bill. "I mean, why would she just leave with some stranger?"

"I can be very convincing," said Bill. "It's my job to take people where they don't want to go. This will not be new for me."

"You're not going to hurt her, are you?" asked Mrs. Thompson.

"I generally don't even have to hurt the fugitives that I bring in. I don't think that a little woman will be too difficult," said Bill. "The boyfriend might catch a beating, though. It depends on what I find."

Mr. Thompson got a serious look on his face. "Now, I can't condone violence, Mr. Bill. Jesus taught us to turn the other cheek, and I have to maintain that sentiment. However, I would not be upset if you didn't bring him back with you."

"And what's so bad about him?" Bill asked.

"He lives an immoral life. He drinks He gambles. He was exciting, but Lizzie doesn't need excitement. She needs to be at home with her family. She needs to be a respectable girl," said Mrs. Thompson. "It's not acceptable for her to be running off like this."

"And how old is Lizzie?" Bill asked.

"Sixteen-years-old. Almost two years under me," said Katy.

"Well, thank you all so much for the meal and the hospitality. I think that I should be heading to sleep as soon as possible. I want to be sure to leave early in the morning."

"Absolutely. You can sleep in Lizzie's bed for the night. It's next to Katy's. Katy will sleep with us in our room tonight. She can show you where your bed is."

Katy showed Bill the small bed in a small room in the house. "It's not much, but it will do," Katy said giving him pillows.

The next morning, Mrs. Thompson had a nice sack of food and other supplies. As he was getting ready to head out, he saw Katy running in from doing her chores.

"Mama! Wait!"

"What is it, child?"

"Mama, I want to go with."

Chapter Three: A Travel Companion

"You can't be serious," Mrs. Thompson said.

"Mama, please. I know she'll come home if I go with," said Katy.

"And who do you suppose is going to do your chores while you're gone?" asked Mrs. Thompson.

"Mama, I haven't gone anywhere in my whole life. Lizzie just ran off. I just want to go with to get her. To see something new," said Katy.

"I'm not having my second daughter run away too," said Mr. Thompson walking out the front door. "I say we let her go. There's only one problem, Katy."

"What's that, pa?"

"The decision isn't really up to us. You'd be a burden on Bill here. Now, that's not really fair to him is it?"

Bill didn't know how to respond. The girl would be a complete burden. She would slow him down, and she would use up his rations. He would have to protect her the whole time, too. "It can get pretty dangerous out there, little lady. I ride fast, too."

"I can ride faster!" she said quickly. "I've been riding these guys since I was young. I am the fastest "rider in town."

"I'll have to spend my time looking after you. I don't want to see you get hurt."

"I've never fallen off my horse before. I can't imagine that anyone would try to hurt us. It's a simple trip down to Kansas and back. And I will be a help. Not a burden."

Bill scoffed. He didn't care how pretty Katy was, he knew that she was going to be a hassle on this trip. He could also see that she wasn't going to let go.

"Get ready quickly. I'll also need more pay, of course."

"Of course," Mr. Thompson said. "Naturally, you will be properly compensated."

Bill nodded and looked over at Katy who was simply giddy. "Well, hurry up!" he said.

"Oh, yes. Of course!" she said running inside. When she came back out, Bill could already tell that Katy had too much stuff with her.

"Are you sure you want to carry all of that on a ride all the way to Kansas?"

"I'll be just fine," Katy said stubbornly as she started loading up her horse.

"Just don't come whining to me when the load is too heavy for you."

"Jeez. I said that I got it, didn't I?"

Bill could start to see exactly how this trip was going to go. As they started riding, though, he was pleasantly surprised at how well she could ride. He stayed behind her to make sure that he could keep an eye on her, and she maintained a decent speed the whole time. She didn't even complain much. Bill was worried that she would need to stop for a break every hour. She went a good six hours before even suggesting stopping for a drink of water. Her face was sweaty, and she was clearly very thirsty- she drank quite a bit. It made Bill giggle internally because he knew that she had gone as far as she possibly could before stopping to show him how tough she was. He decided to make a point to suggest small stops for water more often.

"We're gonna ride until sundown and then set up camp," Bill said. "Eat a small bite now, but we'll eat when we're settled."

"Are we going to find a store?"

"We have food. There's no need for that."

"I thought that we just had some bread and some preserves."

"Hopefully, I can catch a rabbit or something. We can have some meat."

Katy didn't complain. They just went ahead and continued riding for the four hours that they had planned. It was just after sun dark, and they found a quiet area to set up camp off of the road.

"We didn't do so bad for the first day. We'll probably get there in another two or three days," Bill said as he built the fire.

"I really do thank you for bringing me along," Katy said.

"Yeah. Just try to keep up the same pace as today, and you won't be too much of an inconvenience," Bill said.

When the fire was burning, he pulled out a small flask of whiskey from his jacket.

"Are you going to drink on this trip?" Katy said, sounding amazed.

"Ma'am, I am bringing you along on my trip. I would ask you to be so kind as to not tell me what I can and cannot do."

Katy went silent.

"So your sister- is she in love with the guy?" Bill finally said.

"I'm sorry?" she asked.

"The guy that your sister ran off with- is she in love with him?"

"I suppose that she thinks that she is. I don't know about if they're actually in love, though. I hope not. That will make this whole ordeal a hell of a lot harder."

"If they are in love, don't you think that they should stay together?"

"I guess we'll have to talk to her about that when we get to Shadow Creek."

The two then turned silent again for some time. Bill wasn't used to having women with him on his trips, and he was happy that Katy wasn't too chatty. He didn't mind the company, though.

"You know I've never been this far out before. It's absolutely beautiful," Katy said. "It's like seeing the world through different eyes. I'm in a different state doing a different job. You get to travel like this all the time?"

"Yep," said Bill.

"You know, I think they have more stars here than in Independence. Or the stars seem brighter. Something just makes them better here."

"Yep," said Bill. He took another swig out of his flask.

"Does that make you fall over? There was this boy in my school, Johnny. He found his daddy's liquor and started drinking it. He fell over in front of everybody. His daddy beat him so badly that he had to sit on a cushion the next day."

"I can handle my liquor," Bill said.

"Well, I think I'm going to head to bed. I might try to count the stars. Thank you again, Mr. Bill." Katy walked up to him and gave him a big hug. It startled Bill at first, but he went ahead and hugged her back. He didn't know how she did it, but she still smelled like horses and flowers.

"Goodnight."

Chapter Four: Beauty

"Watch where you're going!"Bill called out. Katy was going dangerously fast, laughing the whole time. In fact, she was almost going faster than Bill could manage. She seemed to have a true bond with the horse, and they moved as one. They would lean in the same direction and they both seemed to know when they were going to go for a small jump or go around an object.

"I can go slower if it's too fast for you!" the laughing girl called back.

"It's not too fast for me. I'm supposed to keep you safe. I don't need you falling."

"What? I can't hear you. You're getting pretty far behind, Mr. Bill!"

Bill kicked Bonnie to make her go faster, but the horse was going as fast as she could go. Bill kicked Bonnie again, and she got up on her hind legs, neighing. Bill felt a sharp pain as he fell on the dirt ground. He could see the blood scattered in front of him.

He heard Katy running toward him. Once again, she was laughing. "Seriously, if it was too fast for you, you should have said something. I would have slowed down."

Bill was finally able to get up, but he was still feeling some pain.

"I'm not the one who couldn't go faster. It was Bonnie who couldn't go faster. She's getting old."

"Here, let me help you clean up. Let's go back to that stream we passed."

Bill got back on Bonnie (after apologizing for kicking her) and they gently trotted over to the stream.

"Come here. I have a rag," said Katy. As she stood in front of his with the damp cloth,cleaning his wounds, she was amazingly gentle. When she blew softly on the wound, Bill could see that her eyes were the prettiest color of brown that he had ever seen. She maintained a smile the entire time.

"There. You're all better," Katy said. "You want to sit for a minute?"

"Desperately," Bill said. "I'm also starving."

"Well, we can have these biscuits." Katy handed him some biscuits that she had in a napkin in her pocket.

"Are you eating while riding?"

"I try," Katy laughed. "But mostly I keep them to have them ready for Thunder over there. My mama says I spoil him, but he's always been my favorite."

"You are a very good rider."

"It's my favorite thing in the whole wide world. It makes me feel at one with nature. At one with God. I'd kinda lost that feeling lately, but this trip really helped make me remember how much I love riding Thunder."

"Bonnie's been with me since I was young. It was my first horse, and I took care of her more than I took care of myself. I'd be dirty, but she'd be spotless," Bill said.

"How old is she?"

"She is almost fifteen years old," Bill said. "I'm planning on leaving her with my mom and getting a young stud, but I just can't bare to part with her."

"You'll still see her all of the time," said Katy. "Well, is it time to get back to it? We have a long way to go still."

"Yeah," Bill said. "Let's get going."

They rode at the same pace as the day before and continued through the wilderness. The further they got, the more distracted Katy got by the sites.

"Are those buffalo? Look! I think that there are buffalo down there."

"The town has an entire shop just for ice cream?"

Bill knew that he had to focus on the job at hand, so he kept the mesmerized girl on track. They didn't stop once, although he secretly wanted to show her the sights as much as she wanted to see them. He never wanted to do that before. Could this girl be having an effect on him?

They continued traveling until sundown. Their routine was very similar to their routine the night before. They set up camp off of the road, Bill created a fire, and they had dinner by the fire. Bill noticed that Katy was a little closer to him than she was the night before.

"Tell me about yourself, Bill."

"What's there to tell? I grew up in St. Louis. My dad was gone when I was little. I work to help take care of my ma and my horses."

"Do you have a wife?"

"Nope."

"Do you ever want a wife?"

"I never thought about it before."

"Have you ever kissed a woman?"

"Plenty of times."

"You scoundrel!"

"Not at all. It just never works out."

"Do you like your job?"

"Yep."

"Are you ever lonely?"

"Not really. No."

"Do you think that I'm pretty?"

"Yep. You look fine."

They both went back to eating until they finished their dinner. Katy immediately got up to clean the supplies before bed. Bill sat back and sipped on his whiskey until she came back.

"'The stars are amazing again tonight."

"I reckon they are."

"How many stars do you think there are?"

"Millions. Maybe more."

"I'm just going to lay here and watch the stars."

"That sounds nice."

Katy laid down on the ground next to Bill. She gently laid her head against his shoulder. They sat in silence, and she stared at the stars. Bill hoped that she couldn't feel his heart beating a little more quickly than normal while she was so close. They laid there together for a good twenty minutes.

"I think I'm going to head to bed now," Katy said. And she got up and kissed Bill softly. Bill was shocked but received her kiss tenderly. Her lips were the softest that he had ever felt. "Goodnight."

Chapter Five: A Gift

"Let's get going!" called out Bill. "If we hurry up, we will be able to get there tonight."

"You really think so?" asked Katy.

"It's a stretch but maybe. If not, we'll be very close. We can get there early tomorrow."

"This wasn't so bad!"

"This wasn't that far of a ride. Trust me, it can be quite grueling."

"I believe you! I am starting to feel it in my legs."

They continued to ride through the countryside together only stopping for water and short breaks. Bill started to get excited for even those short times with the beautiful girl. She was pretty, she was funny, and she was tough. Most importantly, he hadn't felt quite so alive as he did on this trip with her. He felt privileged to even be able to drink water next to her. He wasn't sure how to interpret the kiss from the night before. They had not talked about the kiss at all, and it was the only thing that Bill could think about.

It was still light when they got to a small town.

"Hey, let's stop here for awhile," Bill said.

"Can we get some candy maybe?" asked Katy.

"We might be able to do that."

They tied up their horses and started walking around the small town. People were outside, and it was a gorgeous night out. Katy's hair was in her usual long braid that always had some wild strands framing her face.

"So were you just tired?" Katy asked.

"Naw. I saw this little town and thought we might enjoy some civilization."

"Well, you have me with you!"

"And you're wonderful company. I also wouldn't mind some candy, though."

"Look! There's the general store. I'm sure my folks will give you an extra couple of dollars for anything you buy me on the trip."

"I'm not worried about it," Bill said.

The general store was larger than most small town general stores. It had a large selection of everything from food, cigarettes, tools, animal feed, crafts, Bibles, clothing, and jewelry.

"Look at that Bible! It's absolutely beautiful!" said Katy. She ran to an ornate Bible with bold colors and fantastic pictures. Katy flipped through the Bible excitedly. This is the most beautiful thing that I had ever seen!"

"It's quite stunning."

"I wonder how much it is."

"More than we have," Bill said. "It sure is nice, though. They have a lot of nice things at this store."

"I know! Look at that bracelet. That looks like real silver. Do you think that there's real silver in there?"

"I think so. And it looks like there is turquoise, too."

"It's the most beautiful thing that I had ever seen. Oh, the other girls in town would be so jealous if they saw me wearing this. This is better than most wedding rings."

"Let's get back to the candy."

Bill and Katy looked through the numerous cartons of candies and picked out a couple of bags full to take with them. Bill also went ahead and bought a coca cola for them to share outside before riding more.

"Well, we should probably get headed out," Bill said.

"Yep. I'm glad that you suggested stopping here, though."

"Go get the horses ready and I'll be right there, OK?"

"Yes, sir."

Bill waited until Katy was out of view before going into the store to buy the silver bracelet and the Bible.

They rode on until they couldn't see anymore and set up camp.

"Are we close?" asked Katy.

"We'll make it by tomorrow."

"Great. I'm so excited to see my sister."

"She'll be happy to see you, too. I think it will definitely help in getting her to come home."

"I hope that she's not with that good for nothing man of hers anymore."

"Did you save her any pieces of candy?" Bill asked.

Katy had her last piece of candy in her hand and threw it into her mouth and shrugged. "I came all the way out here to come get her. Not bring her candy."

After they had a small dinner, Katy took care of their supplies again. She was very good at keeping things clean. When she got back, she immediately sat very close to Bill and put his arm around her.

"I like watching the stars with you," Bill said.

Katy shushed him and continued looking up into the sky. While she sat with his arm around her, she linked fingers with him. Bill loved the feel of her soft, small fingers in between his.

After a couple of minutes, Bill took her face in his hands and brought her in for their second kiss. She leaned in for more, but Bill leaned back.

"I got you something," he said .

"You have more candy?"

"I think you might like it a little more than that." Bill went into his pocket and pulled out the silver and turquoise bracelet that Katy had loved so much in the store.

Katy's eyes lit up. "It can't be! Bill, I- I love it. Oh, but we have to take it back. My parents will never let me have it. It costs too much. They can't pay you back."

"No. This is from me. I want you to have it."

"Are you sure?"

"I'm very sure."

Katy started to tear up, and she immediately took the bracelet and put it on. "It's the most beautiful thing in the whole wide world!" she screamed. She then wrapped her arms around Bill's neck and passionately kissed him.

"You can't wear it while you're riding," Bill said.

"I know."

"It's for church and when you have company over and all."

"OK"

"And you have to clean it once a month."

"Oh, please just kiss me."

Chapter Six: Lizzie Thompson

The sun lit Katy up like an angel. Bill had woken up early to get to Shadow Creek as soon as possible, and Katy was still sleeping in her blankets.

"Good morning!"

Katy woke up in a bit of a daze.

"It's not even light out yet."

"We're getting an early start. We don't want to get to your sister any later than we have to."

Katy and Bill were on the trail before anyone else that morning. They traveled with purpose, and they traveled quickly.

"How long do you think that it will take us?" Katy asked.

"It will probably be about four hours. Maybe six. I'm hoping that we get there by noon."

At their first stop to let the horses drink water, Bill couldn't help but cuddle with Katy on the river bank.

They continued riding throughout the morning enjoying the breeze hitting their face and continually exchanged jokes throughout the ride. They even raced a little bit across one clear meadow.

"We're coming up to Shadow Creek!" Bill screamed.

"We are?"

"Yep! We'll be with your sister soon enough!"

Bill was right- they rode up to the town shortly after. It was another small town. It wouldn't be too hard to find Lizzie.

"Can I put my bracelet on while we're in town?"

"Don't be silly. It's for Sunday and special occasions. You'll wear it to church the next time you go."

"Well, I'm showing Lizzie. Now, how do we find her?"

"Let's start by asking at the general store. Everybody in town has to shop there."

The couple went into the store and Katy immediately started running.

"Lizzie!" she screamed. Lizzie was there at the general store. It was the perfect timing.

Bill watched the two girls embrace before introducing him.

"Hi, Lizzie. I'm Bill. I came down here with Katy to get you."

"I'll tell you everything after I'm done scolding her for running off in the first place. What were you thinking? What about ma and pa?"

"I'm so sorry, Katy. And I'm so glad that you're here. He's awful. He's absolutely awful."

"What did he do to you, Lizzie? Does he beat you?"

"Once. He drinks and yells a lot, though. I made a horrible mistake. I need to go home."

"Well, mama and papa are going to be happy to have you back. But we gotta go tell him that you're leaving."

"He's gone for the day. I don't want to wait to tell him. I just want to take the horse and go now. I'll leave a note."

Bill, Katy, and Lizzie went back to Lizzie's small home to leave a note for the man that she was leaving. Bill didn't want to get too involved, but he was secretly very happy that he could bring Lizzie back to her family and away from the abusive boyfriend. He was also just happy to see how relieved Katy was.

It didn't take long for the three to start to head back to Independence. The girls spent a good portion of the first day of the trip talking in secret. Bill could only assume that it was girl talk about him. When they set up camp for the night, he immediately put his arm around Katy in front of her sister.

Lizzie started teasing them and asked desperately to see the bracelet that Katy had been going on about. He brought out the bracelet and started realizing that he could truly enjoy a life with Katy. There was only one very important thing to do first.

They made it back in four days. The sun was going down, but no one wanted to camp another night. They pushed through until they finally saw the small gorgeous house with the blue shutters. Bill followed the girls as they excitedly put their horses away and got ready to surprise their parents.

Mr and Mrs. Thompson were in the main room by the fire when they walked in. They had huge smiles and both ran to Lizzie to greet her.

"Oh, honey. Why would you do that to us? I'm so glad that you're home," said Mrs. Thompson, hugging her daughter.

"Lizzie, you have a lot of chores to make up," Mr. Thompson said.

"Let her relax at least for the night," said Mrs. Thompson. "You put your stuff away and clean up and relax tonight. You are going to be worked pretty hard in the morning, though."

"I can't thank you enough for bringing our daughter back home to us," Mr. Thompson told Bill.

"It was truly my pleasure, sir. Your daughters are both amazing people. In fact, Katy and I got really close on the trip-"

"Daddy! Bill bought Katy the prettiest ring I've ever seen! And she said that they kissed!" Lizzie blurted.

Mr. Thompson gave Katy and Bill a suspicious look for a moment. "I assume that you are a good person if you were sent here by Sheriff O'Malley. I look forward to getting to know you while you court my daughter."

Katy looked relieved. "Oh, thank you, daddy. Thank you! Let me show you the bracelet."

"Thank you very much, sir. I really was hoping for your approval. I also got a small present for you as well. I know that you're a man of God, so I thought that it would be a nice addition for either the home or the church," said Bill.

"What are you talking about?" Katy asked.

"I didn't tell you, but I got your dad a gift, too. I wanted to ask for the right to court you properly. I'll be right back."

Bill came back with the elaborate Bible that he and Katy had seen at the General Store. The whole family was in awe, and everyone passed the beautiful book around.

"This will be the nicest Bible at the church," Mr. Thompson said.

"Come on, sweetheart," Katy said. "Let's go look at the stars."